THE *LILY*

SECRET MONEY

D0681552

LOIS GLADYS LEPPARD

MOORINGS

NASHVILLE, TENNESSEE

A DIVISION OF THE BALLANTINE PUBLISHING GROUP,
RANDOM HOUSE, INC.

The Lily Adventures™
SECRET MONEY

Library of Congress Cataloging-in-Publication Data

Leppard, Lois Gladys
    Secret Money / Lois Gladys Leppard. — 1st ed.
        p.   cm. — (The Lily Adventures ; 1)
    Summary: In 1901, sixteen-year-old Lily Masterson, traveling in England with her young sister, receives a note and enough money to return to South Carolina, where her Christian beliefs strengthen her as she investigates the death of her father.
    ISBN: 0-345-39576-X (pbk.)
    [1. Christian Life—Fiction.   2. Mystery and detective stories.]
I. Title.   II. Series: Leppard, Lois Gladys.   Lily adventures ; 1.
PZ7.L556Se   1995
[Fic]—dc20
95-7464
CIP
AC

First Edition: April 1995

10   9   8   7   6   5   4   3   2   1

Ask, and it shall be given you.

—Matthew 7:7 (King James Version)

This book is dedicated with love and thanks
to
all those readers who have grown up with
MANDIE.

Contents

Chapter One
Bound for Home

The tiny room was pitch dark. The roar of the storm raging outside was deafening. The bunk seemed to turn this way and that as the ship fought with the angry waves.

Lily held one arm around her six-year-old sister to keep her from being flung from the bed, and with her other hand she tightly grasped the post above her pillow. Even though the heavy rain had cooled the warm September weather, Violet was wet with perspiration from fright.

"I love you," Lily told her as she gave Violet a squeeze.

"Me, too," Violet managed to reply in a hoarse, tearful voice.

Lily was not feeling too well herself. She realized the danger they were in. The ship was somewhere in the middle of the Atlantic Ocean, hundreds of miles from land. If the storm tore the vessel apart there was not much chance of survival. And it was also the middle of the night. She had been awakened when Violet came down from the upper bunk to crawl in beside her.

Violet twisted to glance up at Lily in the darkness. Her voice trembled as she tried to speak above the noise. "Do you remember Mandie Shaw?" she asked.

Lily was surprised at the question. "Why, yes, dear, I do remember Mandie Shaw," she replied with her mouth next to

Violet's ear to make herself heard. "She was on the ship with us when we went to stay with Aunt Emma in England."

"Remember that bad storm we had on the ship then, and Mandie told us how afraid she was?" Violet asked.

"Yes, I remember," Lily said. "And you know we got through that storm all right, so I think we'll be all right this time, too."

"I wish we could just hurry up and get home. I want to see Papa," Violet said as her breath caught in her throat.

"I know, dear," Lily said, pushing back the child's damp blonde hair. She had not told Violet that their father was ill and that was why they were going home. The money for their fare had arrived at Aunt Emma's last week accompanied by a message, "Come home at once. Your father ill." It had been signed by someone named Weyman Braddock and was dated September 2, 1901.

"You must go at once," Aunt Emma had said.

"But I have no idea who this Weyman Braddock is," Lily had argued. "I've never heard the name before. And why is he sending money for our fare home?"

"Lily, now is not the time to go into all this," Aunt Emma said. "We will make arrangements for you girls to sail on the first ship to the United States. You can find out who this person is when you arrive home. He's probably a friend of your father."

Lily was more worried about her father's health than the strange name, so she packed her and Violet's things and got ready to sail.

Now, during this storm, Lily was desperately hoping they would make it home to her father.

A sudden *slam-bang* outside their room caused both girls to sit up in alarm. Lily hit her head on the upper bunk but hardly noticed, so great was her fright. *Was the ship being torn apart?* she wondered. She listened, but the sound was not repeated.

Violet, clinging to her, tried to talk between sobs. "Lily, it's so dark—in here—I can't see," she said.

"I know, but all the lights are out," Lily replied. They were in an inside room without a porthole, and on calm nights she left a small lamp burning on the table in the corner because Violet would be frightened if she happened to wake in the dark. But during this storm, a lighted lamp would be dangerous.

The storm seemed to quiet down a little, and Lily could hear someone moving about in the corridor outside. Suddenly she got a glimpse of light through the crack under their door. She quickly pushed around Violet, jumped out of the bunk, and ran to the door. She opened it far enough to peek out and saw a man carrying a lantern going past.

Lily, with the door only partly open because she was not dressed, called to him, "Mister! Do you know what that loud racket was just now? It sounded like it was outside our door." Violet had followed her and was clinging to the back of her nightgown.

The man turned back to look at Lily, and she could see he was a young man, tall, thin, and well-dressed.

"No, I was looking for the source of the disturbance myself," he said as he came back toward her. "You see, I have the room next to yours."

The ship suddenly gave a lurch, throwing Violet backward. Her grasp on Lily's skirt pulled Lily with her. Lily managed to balance herself by holding on to the door, but the door itself had opened all the way and she realized she was standing there in her nightclothes in the light of the man's lantern.

"I'm sorry," she said, and she practically slammed the door in the stranger's face. She leaned against the closed door and hoped she would not meet up with the man during the rest of their voyage.

Violet had crawled back into bed and, as Lily joined her, the child asked, "Lily, who was that man?"

"I don't know, Violet," Lily told her as they snuggled up together. "Just some passenger on the ship."

"I didn't like him," Violet said.

"Why, Violet! You don't even know him. How can you say that?" Lily asked. "I thought he was nice-looking."

Violet shook her head as she said, "No, no, he had untrustable eyes."

Lily laughed softly as she replied, "He had nice brown eyes, I believe."

"Oh, but they were squinty, and Papa always says don't trust squinty-eyed people," Violet said firmly.

"Well, we probably won't see him again anyway," Lily replied. She suddenly realized the storm seemed to have subsided. The roar was gone, and after that one lurch that had opened her door, the ship had steadied itself. She gave a big sigh of relief.

Violet had noticed, too, and she sat up. "I'll get back in my bed now, Lily. You're too big. You take up all the room," she said as she quickly climbed the ladder to the upper bunk. "Good night."

Lily smiled to herself and replied, "Good night, sweet dreams, dear." Her little sister answered with only a grunt. She was already falling asleep.

Although the storm seemed to be over, Lily tossed and turned most of the night. So many things were on her mind.

She felt her face grow warm when she remembered standing in her nightgown in front of the stranger. She couldn't ever remember feeling so embarrassed. He had seemed a little older than her sixteen years and was really not bad-looking in spite of Violet's description of him. But after meeting him that way, she hoped she would be able to avoid him the rest of the trip home.

Home—she couldn't get home fast enough. Ships took so long to cross from Europe to the United States. Why couldn't someone build one that would go faster? And the vessel they were on was much smaller than the great *Victoria* they had sailed on to Europe. Therefore, it would take longer.

The message they had received only said that her father was ill. She had no idea what was wrong with him or how sick he really was. And he was all alone now that her mother had died the previous summer. He had insisted that she and Violet go to stay with their Aunt Emma in England because he was badly in debt from her mother's long illness, and he had been sure Aunt Emma could better provide for them.

"Oh, Papa, I didn't want to go," Lily whispered to herself.

She remembered the terrible steerage section she and Violet

had traveled in. And Violet had become ill with the fever, and Mandie Shaw had talked her grandmother, Mrs. Taft, into moving Violet to the sick bay in spite of protests from the captain.

Mandie had promised to get in touch with them later, but Lily had never heard a word from her. When they arrived in England, Lily discovered that Mandie's grandmother actually owned the *Victoria*, so she didn't expect to ever hear from her again. She and Violet were daughters of a blacksmith, far below the status of Mandie's family. But she would always have a warm spot in her heart for Mandie. Without her help, Violet might have died.

And if Mandie's white cat, Snowball, had not run away and come down into the steerage section where Violet had immediately claimed him, they would never have met. Lily smiled to herself as she remembered how determined Violet had been to keep Snowball. Mrs. Taft had given her money to buy a kitten when they reached London—a white one if possible—but Lily had not been able to find a kitten that Violet wanted. Instead, she chose a white spitz that was for sale on the farm adjoining her Aunt Emma's property. And now the puppy was traveling home with them in the baggage room below.

"Oh, stop this, Lily, and go to sleep," she whispered to herself. She turned to face the door. There was light coming in through the crack at the bottom. This time it was a steady light, indicating the lights were back on in the corridor.

The next thing Lily knew, Violet was standing by her bunk. "Lily, time to get up," the child said as she reached to shake her.

Lily quickly sat up, bumped her head on the upper bunk, and swung her feet to the floor as she rubbed the pained place.

"Goodness!" Lily exclaimed. "It sure got to be morning fast, didn't it?" She rose and began dressing. She put on a new lavender voile dress she had made in England.

Violet put on her clothes in a big hurry. "I'm hungry!" she told Lily. "I'm glad it did get morning in a hurry."

Lily buttoned up Violet's dress and tied her sash. Then she brushed her little sister's long blonde hair and tied it back with a ribbon. She stood back and looked at Violet. "I think you'll pass," Lily told her teasingly.

"You, too, Lily, but let's go eat," Violet insisted. She never seemed to care about anything but food. Clothes were not important to her, even though Lily had made the frilly lacy pink dress she had on.

Since they were in the second-class section of the ship, the girls dined in a small dining room separate from the wealthy first-class passengers. As soon as they entered the room, Lily spotted the man they had seen in the corridor the night before. She tried to ignore him, but he had seen them, too, and waved for the girls to join him at his table.

Not knowing what else to do, Lily led Violet to his table. When the child saw who was at the table, she pulled away from Lily's hand and climbed into a chair on the other side of the table so that Lily had to take the vacant chair next to the man.

"Good morning," the man said. "I'm glad to see you've survived the storm." He pulled out the chair and waited for her to be seated.

"Yes, thank you," Lily replied, still not able to look directly at him as she remembered the scene the night before. She suddenly realized she didn't even know his name and she looked sharply at him as she asked, "Would you please tell me who you are? I know we talked last night, but I don't think I got your name."

The man sat down next to her and said, "I'm sorry. My name is Wilbur Whitaker and I'm on my way home to the United States—to South Carolina, in fact. My family has just moved there from Michigan."

"My name is Lily Masterson, and this is my little sister, Violet, and we are also on our way home to South Carolina," Lily replied. "What—"

"I know," he interrupted. "You live in the country near Fountain Inn, and our family lives in town."

Lily quickly looked at him, surprised. "Well, how did you learn all that?"

"I saw you on deck yesterday and asked a crewman to find out who you were," he said quickly, without looking at her. "Besides, we're next-door neighbors."

Lily looked at him again. She had not been wrong the night before. He was nice-looking, with brown eyes, brown curly hair, and a smile that showed perfect white teeth. But there was something about him that didn't ring true, and she couldn't figure out what it was. She glanced at Violet and saw that she was staring at the man and frowning.

"How long has your family been in Fountain Inn, Mr. Whitaker?" Lily asked as a waiter brought food and placed it on their table.

"Oh, only a few weeks," Wilbur replied. "And please call me Wilbur. Mr. Whitaker sounds too formal, doesn't it? And like I said, we *are* neighbors." He looked at her and smiled as he reached for a platter of scrambled eggs and passed it to her.

Lily shrugged, then helped herself to the eggs and turned to put some on Violet's plate as well.

"You said you were hungry," Lily told the child as she gave her a generous portion.

"Yes, I am," Violet said, finally taking her gaze off Wilbur Whitaker to look at her plate. "And some bacon, please, and a biscuit, and lots of marmalade." She licked her lips in anticipation as Lily added each of her requests.

"That was quite a storm we had last night," Wilbur said as he filled his plate. "I understand it shook up some baggage in the room across from yours. That was the noise we heard; things weren't securely packed down."

"I'm glad to know what it was," Lily said as she began eating. She was not comfortable with the man when she thought about what had happened the night before. Now she wished she had ignored him and sat somewhere else.

Violet ate hungrily, but Lily noticed she kept watching Wilbur. The man had ignored Violet, and Lily knew her sister didn't like to be ignored. She almost held her breath, afraid of what Violet might say or do since she had already said she didn't like the man.

"I hope we don't have another storm before we reach Charleston," Wilbur said as he dug into his food.

"So do I," Lily replied. She couldn't relax enough to try to carry on a conversation with him. And he didn't seem very talkative either.

Lily watched Violet as she cleaned off her plate and turned her attention back to Wilbur. She tried to think of something to talk about so the child wouldn't have a chance to say something that might show her disapproval of the man.

Then Lily remembered the name on the message that had come with the money for her fare and wondered if Wilbur might know the man. "Have you met anyone named Weyman Braddock in or around Fountain Inn since your family moved there?" she asked.

Wilbur looked at her quickly and asked, "Who?"

"Weyman Braddock," Lily told him.

"Weyman Braddock . . . ," Wilbur repeated the name. "No, I don't believe I have. What does he do?"

"I have no idea," Lily said. "I've never heard of him. But his name was on the message I received in England telling me I should come home immediately because my father was ill. I just don't know who Mr. Braddock is."

"I'm sorry if your father is ill, but I don't know the man either," Wilbur replied as he picked up his cup to sip the coffee.

Violet had been listening to the conversation and now turned anxious blue eyes toward Lily as she asked, "Papa is sick?"

Lily leaned to pat Violet's small hand as she said, "Yes, sweetie pie, but don't you worry. We're on the way home to see him."

"Is that man with the you-know-what eyes going home with us?" Violet asked as she indicated Wilbur with her eyes.

"No, Violet. Let's finish our food now and we'll go for a walk on the deck," Lily quickly replied. She wouldn't look at Wilbur.

"May I join you girls on the deck?" Wilbur asked. He folded his napkin and laid it beside his plate, then gave Violet a curious look.

"No!" Violet spoke sharply.

"Violet, please watch your manners," Lily said. Then turning to Wilbur, she explained. "You see, I've practically raised her myself. My mother was ill from the time Violet was born and never was able to look after her up until she died this past summer."

Wilbur cleared his throat and said, "I'm sorry."

As the three stood up to leave the table, Lily reached for Violet's hand and tried to keep her by her side, away from Wilbur. When the young man came to walk on her other side she realized how tall he was. At five feet and five inches, she was considered tall for a woman, but Wilbur seemed a foot taller.

Wilbur looked down at her as they left the dining room and asked, "Do you mind if I walk with you and your sister on the deck?"

Lily couldn't think up any excuse in a hurry. She knew Violet might unexpectedly say or do something irritating to him. And she herself was not very comfortable around him. They walked on toward the outside door that led to the deck.

"Well, of course," Lily replied as they stepped out onto the deck. "If you want to walk with us, we'd be glad to have you come along. We won't stay outside long though because we didn't get much sleep last night."

"I agree," Wilbur said. "A little nap would be nice but, you know, I've always heard lost sleep can never be replaced." He grinned and looked down at her.

"Well, I suppose that it's impossible, to replace lost sleep, that is, but I know a little nap can be refreshing after losing sleep," Lily said with a smile. "I've lost a lot of sleep looking after Violet and my mother while she was ill, and I've learned naps are sometimes necessary."

"Yes, you've probably had your hands full," Wilbur said as they walked on.

Lily was curious as to how he occupied his time, so she asked, "And what do you do for a living?"

"For a living?" Wilbur looked shocked. "Well, I have to admit that I don't have to work for a living because my family has money, but I intend finding something to occupy me now that we've moved south. Maybe I'll go back to school to study law. Or maybe I'll buy myself a farm and raise horses. Or maybe I'll find something else even more interesting. Who knows? I'm just testing the waters right now, so to speak."

"Must be nice to just be lazy," Lily said with a shrug. "But some people still have to work and some people do enjoy work. Count me in the last. I couldn't stand not working."

The sun was shining brightly, and the deck was crowded. Lily held tighter to Violet's hand because she was afraid she might break loose and run off. But Violet looked up at Lily and said, "You don't have to hold my hand so tight, Lily. I'm not going to run away. Can we go downstairs and see my puppy, please?"

"No, Violet, that's impossible," Lily replied. "Remember the man said he would take care of your puppy until we get off the ship. Then you can have him."

"But, Lily, why can't we go see that man and ask him how my puppy is?" Violet looked up, begging with her big blue eyes.

"Violet, there's no use in arguing about this now," Lily said as she stopped to bend over to speak to the child. "We talked about this when we got on the ship, remember?"

"Oh, Lily, this ship goes so slow that my puppy may not even remember me when we get home," Violet argued.

"I'm sure he'll know you and will be following you everywhere you go when we get home. Now I think it's time for us to go take a nap," Lily said, straightening up to look at Wilbur. "I'd better take her to our room."

"Sorry you have to go inside, but then maybe I'll go to my room and catch a quick snooze, too," Wilbur said, following along with Lily and Violet as they walked back to the door.

Lily wondered why Wilbur wanted to stay right with her on every move she made. He didn't seem romantically inclined and he didn't talk a whole lot. He just seemed to stick to her and Violet like molasses, and she was not happy about it. Lily was silent until they reached the door of her cabin. Then she turned and said, "I've enjoyed the walk, but I have some other things to do right now."

"I've enjoyed it, too," Wilbur said, moving back to his door. "See you later."

Lily and Violet stepped into their cabin and Lily said under her breath, "See you later? No, I hope not!"

Violet looked at her questioningly. "What?"

"Let's remove your nice new dress so you won't wrinkle it, and then you jump up there in your bunk and take a nap," Lily said, bending to unbutton the garment.

"You, too?" Violet asked as she stepped out of her skirt.

"Well, yes. Me, too," Lily said while hanging up the dress. "I'll get in my bunk, too, but I think I'll write in my journal. I have to record everything so Papa can read about what we've been doing since we left home."

Violet climbed up and lay down with her face hanging over the edge so she could watch her sister.

Lily removed her dress and slipped into a robe. She pulled her notebook and a pencil out of a valise and propped up her pillows. She sat on her bunk and tried to think where she should begin. Her recordings were up to date as of last evening, so now she must begin with the storm during the night.

She read what she was writing in a low voice, "Terrible storm. Met the man in the cabin next door, Wilbur Whitaker." She continued through the events of the morning and then stopped to think about the man named Wilbur Whitaker.

He was certainly different from the fellows she knew back home. Most of them were about her own age and were full of flattery. They all seemed to have a contest going as to who would be the first to come calling. Papa didn't think she was old enough to have young men visiting her. But she had not really had time for young men anyway, because she had been tied up with helping her mother and Violet. And she had just reached sixteen on the previous July sixth. Now maybe Papa would allow it.

"But no one is coming calling until the right one comes along," Lily said aloud to herself as she closed her notebook, dropped it and the pencil over the side onto the floor, and then curled up for a nap.

She had just begun to feel sleepy and relaxed when there was a tap on her door. Frowning, she remembered to duck her head as she sat up. She slipped out of the bunk and hurried to the door.

Remembering that she was not dressed, she called through the door, "Who is it?" She looked back at Violet, who was sound asleep now, and hoped she wouldn't wake up.

"Lily Masterson?" a man's voice questioned outside the door.

"Yes, what is it?" she asked.

"Lily, it's me, Ossie Creighton," the man said.

"Oh, Ossie, wait a minute. I have to get dressed," Lily said, and she quickly turned to put her dress back on.

"All right," Ossie agreed.

She buttoned her dress, wondering what Ossie Creighton was doing on the ship. She had not seen him on board, but since they had not made any stops for passengers to embark, he must have been on the vessel all along. Ossie was a young widower who lived on the farm next to her father's land. Lily had known him all her life. He had always been like a big brother, and she was overjoyed to find a friend like Ossie for the rest of the journey home.

She smoothed her blonde hair as she opened the door and slipped out into the corridor. She motioned to show him that Violet was asleep as she closed the door softly behind her.

Lily had always heard other people say Ossie was ugly as homemade sin but she had always thought she had never seen a kinder face. He had helped her through many childhood troubles growing up. He married a local girl when Lily was five years old, but his young wife died a year later with tuberculosis. Then it had been Lily's turn to comfort him in her childlike way. The role was reversed when Lily was ten and Violet was born, when her mother became an invalid. Ossie had taken over like a big brother and was there for her when Lily's mother died that last summer.

Ossie adjusted his spectacles on his nose and smiled at Lily. "I'm so happy you're on this boat," he said. He wasn't much taller than Lily and was a little overweight.

"Ossie, I'm so glad to see you," Lily replied. "I have to just stand here and talk because I can't leave Violet alone in the room."

"I understand," Ossie said. "But what are you and Violet doing on this ship? I take it you're going home."

"Yes, we got a message that Papa was ill," Lily began explaining, and then she quickly asked, "Have you seen Papa lately? Do you know if he is ill?"

"No, I haven't seen him recently, Lily," Ossie replied. "You see, I'm going home, too. I've been to England on business—cotton business, that is—for Mr. Dutton. I left just a few days after you and Violet went to Europe."

"Traveling for Mr. Dutton all the way to England? Ossie, you must have been given more responsibility," Lily said with a big smile.

Ossie worked in Mr. Dutton's office in Fountain Inn but lived on his farm and hired workers to tend it.

Ossie grinned at her behind his dark mustache and replied, "Well, you know Mr. Dutton. I may have responsibility in one thing one day, but he may change my duties the next day. Nevertheless, he is a good man to work for and a good teacher. So one day I hope to learn enough to set up my own cotton business."

"I don't think that will be far away either," Lily said with a smile. Then she remembered the name on the message she had received. Perhaps Ossie would have heard of the man. "Ossie, we got this message signed by someone named Weyman Braddock saying Papa was ill and we should come home immediately. Do you know anyone by that name?"

"Weyman Braddock," Ossie said thoughtfully. "No, I don't believe I've ever heard of the man. And you say he sent you a message to come home."

"Yes, and he even sent the money for our fare," Lily said. "It couldn't be a joke of some kind, could it? I've been so worried not knowing what is wrong with Papa."

"That is really puzzling," Ossie said. "Weyman Braddock. I just can't place the name at all. And he said your father was ill.

He must be someone who knows your father, wouldn't you say?"

"I suppose," Lily replied. "But I've never heard my father mention that name that I can recollect." She looked at him with a worried expression. "I'll be so glad when this journey ends."

Ossie patted her shoulder and said, "Let me think on this awhile. I'm traveling alone. Would you and Violet join me in the dining room at noon, and we'll discuss this further."

"Of course," Lily agreed. "We'll meet you at the door at twelve sharp."

"I'll see you then," Ossie said as he walked on down the corridor.

Lily silently opened the door and went back inside her cabin. She stooped to pick up her journal and the pencil where she had left them on the floor when Violet came sliding down the ladder from her bunk.

"You scared me!" Lily teased her little sister.

"I haven't been asleep," Violet told her as she stretched.

"Not much," Lily continued teasing.

"I know you went outside in the hall to talk to someone—probably that squinty-eyed man," Violet replied with a grin.

"Wrong," Lily said as she took Violet's dress down from the hanger. "Guess who it was?" She paused, but Violet remained silent. "It was Ossie, and we're going to eat with him!"

"Ossie? He's really and truly on this boat?" Violet was excited.

"Yep, and he's been on this boat ever since we got on in England," Lily replied, helping Violet into her dress.

Violet, puzzled, looked at her and asked, "Well, if he's been on this boat all that time why haven't we seen him?"

"Well, there are a lot of people on here, and I suppose we just didn't see each other until now," Lily said, buttoning the dress and then adding thoughtfully, "But if he didn't know we were on here, how did he know we were in this room?"

"Did you ask him?" Violet inquired.

"No, but I can guarantee you I will ask him just that when we meet him for the noon meal," Lily replied as she continued buttoning Violet's dress.

Lily thought about that while she dressed herself. *How did Ossie know we were in this room if he didn't even know we were on the ship? I'm going to find out.*

Chapter Two
Squinty Eyes

Even though Lily and Violet were fifteen minutes early to meet Ossie at the dining room door, he was already there. Violet immediately took possession of him. She grabbed his hand and began telling him all about England.

"Violet, let's go inside and sit down first before you go into all that," Lily told her, smiling at Ossie as they moved through the doorway.

Ossie grasped Violet's hand and led the way to a table.

"You know, Violet, I knew you would enjoy your visit with your aunt in England," Ossie told her as he helped her up into a chair. Then he turned to pull out a seat for Lily and sat down in a chair between them.

"And I've got a white puppy. It's downstairs," Violet continued.

"So you've got yourself a dog," Ossie said. "I'm anxious to see it."

The waiter began placing food on the table, so Lily took the opportunity to distract Violet from going into further detail. "Violet, let's see what we've got to eat here," she said as she looked over the dishes.

Violet immediately began selecting her food. "Some of that,

some of the potatoes, the beans, some biscuits, and, you know, a little of everything," she told her sister.

Lily and Ossie smiled as Lily filled the child's plate. Then the two helped themselves and continued their conversation from where they had left off that morning.

"Lily, I've been racking my brain, but I can't place the name Weyman Braddock," Ossie told her, pausing to sip his coffee. "I've lived around Fountain Inn all my life, but I can't remember ever hearing it. Are you sure that's the name?"

"Oh, yes, Ossie," Lily replied as she laid down her fork for a moment. "I'm positive. I just can't figure out how this man knew where we were and why he sent the message and the money for our fare. I'd think one of my father's sisters would have contacted us if my father is ill."

"Yes, I would think so, too," Ossie agreed. "However, since we don't know the circumstances, we'll just have to wait and see what it's all about."

Lily remembered the question she was going to ask him. "Tell me, Ossie, how did you know we were on this ship and which room we were in?"

Ossie's face reddened slightly, and he looked down at his plate. Then he raised his head and, with a small laugh, replied, "I had to do a little detective work. I happened to see you in the dining room here this morning with a tall young man whom I didn't know. I figured he was some shipboard acquaintance and I'd better find out your room number and give you some brotherly advice."

"Advice? Is there something wrong with that man? His name is Wilbur Whitaker, by the way, and his family just moved to Fountain Inn from Michigan a few weeks ago," Lily told him. "I met him last night during the storm. He has the room next to ours."

"Advice, yes," Ossie said, putting down his cup. "I know you and Violet are on a ship and away from home by yourselves, and I wanted to warn you about talking to strangers." He laughed as though it were a joke.

Lily frowned as she replied, "You know, Ossie, the man is

awfully nice, but he doesn't talk very much. He's also nice-looking, but there's something I can't figure out about him. Why does he even bother to speak to me if he isn't interested in carrying on a conversation?"

"Perhaps he's smitten speechless," Ossie teased.

Lily shrugged and said, "No, he's not."

Violet had been listening and said, "I know what's wrong with that man. He has untrustable eyes, Ossie."

Ossie looked at her with a puzzled expression and asked, "What kind of eyes?"

"Squinty eyes like Papa says we should never trust," Violet explained, then she crammed her mouth full of mashed potatoes.

Ossie smiled and asked Lily, "Would you like for me to check him out with the captain?"

"I don't think that's necessary, Ossie. He has already told me who he is." She picked up a forkful of meat and continued, "He said his family has money and he doesn't have to work. You might be able to find out how they got the money."

"Exactly," Ossie agreed as he sliced a piece of roast. "I'll see what the captain knows."

Lily happened to look across the room and saw Wilbur Whitaker sitting alone in the far corner. She turned her head quickly before he caught her glance.

"The object of our conversation is sitting over there," Lily said, indicating with her eyes the direction to Wilbur's table.

Ossie glanced that way without moving his head. "So he is," he said. "You say he told you his family moved to Fountain Inn a few weeks ago?"

"Yes, that's what he said," Lily replied, putting down her fork and picking up the cup of coffee by her plate.

"And his name is Wilbur Whitaker . . . Whitaker," Ossie repeated the name. "Can't say I've heard about them moving to our town."

"But you've been gone probably a couple of months if you left right after we did," Lily said.

"You know how our town is," Ossie reminded her. "Everybody knows everybody else's business, and if his family is so wealthy, surely they would have purchased a place to live before moving their belongings."

"You're right. He did say they live in town, too," Lily said.

"And I don't know of any houses that were sold recently, or even any that were for sale," Ossie said.

There was a moment of silence as Lily thought about the Whitakers.

"I told you Papa always said, 'Don't trust people with squinty eyes,' " Violet said loudly, in order to get their attention.

"Violet!" Lily gasped and looked around the room, hoping no one had heard the child's sudden remark. "Please don't talk so loud."

Ossie looked at her and smiled. "And does this Mr. Whitaker have squinty eyes, Violet?"

"Oh, yes, he does," she replied seriously. "I warned Lily about him." She looked at her big sister and folded her arms across her chest.

Lily glanced at her plate. "If we're all finished, why don't we go outside where we can walk while we talk?"

"Good idea," Ossie agreed. He stood up and helped Lily rise.

Lily straightened her long skirts and turned to hold Violet's hand. The child had already caught Ossie's coattail, and he reached down to clasp her hand. Lily was glad Violet liked Ossie because she considered him her dearest friend. She was thankful he was on the boat.

"Good afternoon," said a male voice behind her as she was going through the doorway with Ossie and Violet.

Lily recognized it as Wilbur's, and wondered how he had managed to cross the room so swiftly. She looked back with a sweet smile and said, "Good afternoon." Violet had pulled Ossie on ahead.

"I just wanted to know if you and Violet would dine with me tonight," Wilbur said as he looked down at her.

Lily was flustered for a moment, but quickly invented an excuse, "I'm so sorry, but you see, we've met up with an old friend today and we're having supper with him."

"I'm so disappointed," Wilbur said, glancing at Ossie and Violet, who were waiting a few feet away. "Could we make it for breakfast?"

"I'm not sure what we'll be doing in the morning. Perhaps we'll see you later," Lily said. She turned and quickly moved to join Ossie and her sister without even looking back to see where Wilbur went.

"He's an insistent fellow, isn't he?" Ossie remarked as they walked along the deck.

"I'm afraid I told a little lie back there," Lily admitted. "In order to get rid of him I told him we were having supper with you tonight."

"Oh, but that's not a lie, Lily," Ossie said. "I plan on taking up all your time until this ship docks in Charleston."

"Ossie, you don't have to if you have other things to do, you know," Lily said.

"I have nothing else to do but enjoy your company and I'll speak to the captain as soon as I can," Ossie assured her.

Violet jerked on Ossie's hand and looked up at him. "Me, too?"

Ossie playfully jerked back. "Of course, you too," he said with a big smile.

They walked across the deck for a while and then found chairs in the shade and sat down. While Ossie and Lily talked about what they had done and seen in England, Violet began nodding.

"The visit to my aunt's was an educational experience, but I'm so glad to be going home," Lily said. "I didn't want to leave in the first place, but Papa insisted."

"I've always said everybody should have to live in a foreign country for a while, because when they come back, they would really appreciate the United States," Ossie remarked.

"You've always said that? Does that mean this wasn't your first overseas journey?" Lily asked.

"Not my first, but the first in many years," Ossie said. He adjusted his spectacles as he looked at her. "I can remember being moved around the world when I was a toddler. My father was a missionary in six or eight different countries before he died when I was six."

"Ossie!" Lily said with surprise. "I've known you all my life and I never knew that. You always said he was a missionary, but somehow I never realized that meant going to foreign countries. He's buried in your family plot. I've seen his grave."

"Yes, we were home on leave when he came down with pneumonia and didn't recover," Ossie said. "You can remember my mother, I'm sure. She died right before I got married."

"I'm sorry, Ossie. You lost everybody while you were so young," Lily remarked. "You've been alone so long."

"Someday I'll remedy the situation," Ossie said with a big smile. "I'll find someone to love—" He paused.

"And get married again," Lily finished for him. "Oh, Ossie, I hope she's someone I like. You seem to belong to us—Violet and me."

Ossie had a faraway look in his eyes as he replied, "I promise, I'll never marry anyone you don't approve of."

Violet suddenly woke up, shook her head, and said, "Ossie, you're going to get married?"

"No, no. Not right now," Ossie said quickly.

Lily finally noticed how sleepy Violet was. "I think we'd better go take a little nap," she said, standing up.

Ossie rose also, and said, "And while you're doing that I'll see if I can get a word with the captain. Suppose we meet again at the dining room door for supper, around six?"

"We'll be there," Lily promised. She took Violet's hand and led her toward the door.

The corridors inside were practically deserted, and as they moved along, Lily noticed her shoe heels making a loud noise on the wooden floor. Violet more or less dragged her feet.

"Let's hurry before we fall asleep," Lily urged the child as they turned the corner into the hallway where their room was located.

"I won't fall asleep—oh, Lily, look!" Violet suddenly became alert and she pointed ahead.

Lily glanced in that direction and was amazed to see Wilbur Whitaker coming out of their room. She rushed forward to confront him. He stopped in the doorway when he saw her.

"What are you doing?" she demanded, staring angrily into his eyes.

He was fumbling with the door. "I . . . was just looking to see if you were in your room," he practically stuttered. "I . . . thought we might have a chance to talk awhile or walk together on the deck."

Lily put her hands on her hips while Violet clenched her fists.

"You have no right to open my door, much less go into my room," Lily warned him angrily.

"I apologize," Wilbur said as he backed away. "I only glanced inside to see if you were maybe napping. I didn't want to wake you if you were." He backed away down the hallway, turned, and quickly disappeared around the corner.

Violet frowned and stomped her foot. "I told you he had squinty eyes."

"That's enough of that kind of talk. Now, let's get that dress off and you climb up there and take a nap," Lily said firmly when they had entered the room.

Violet didn't protest, and as soon as she was asleep, Lily got out her journal and began recording the day's events in it.

As she wrote, Lily thought about Wilbur Whitaker. She realized she was attracted to him, but there was something not just right. And now, after catching him in her room, she was determined to find out exactly who he was.

Maybe Ossie would be able to get some information from the captain about the man. However, she wondered if the captain knew any more than she did. Evidently Wilbur was only a passenger on the ship, just like she was.

A sudden idea jarred her thoughts. Could Wilbur Whitaker be a detective of some kind? Could he be investigating something or other about her? He didn't seem to be much of a talker, but maybe she could entice him to tell her more about himself and his family if she played sweet and interested. Of course she would have to let Ossie in on her scheme even though she didn't think he would go along with this plan, but it was necessary to try to find out why he had been in her room. Nothing had been disturbed. Evidently her noisy heels had warned him she was coming before he was able to find whatever he had come for.

Lily and Violet went to the dining room early for supper. Lily was so upset about Wilbur she could hardly wait to discuss the incident with Ossie. She had always talked about her problems with him, and he had always given her good advice. But this time she was not so sure Ossie would agree to her plan.

Ossie came hurrying up a few minutes after the girls got to the door. He smiled and led them into the dining room.

"Just wait until you hear what happened after we left you this afternoon," Lily began as soon as the three were seated and the food was placed on the table.

Ossie looked at her in alarm. "What?"

Lily began putting food on Violet's plate so the child would stay out of the conversation.

"More potatoes," Violet told her as she watched.

"All right, plenty of potatoes," Lily agreed, and spooned another helping onto her plate.

She didn't have to tell Violet to eat. The child always seemed to be hungry.

"When Violet and I went to our room after we left you this afternoon," Lily began, "we were almost to our door when we saw that man, Wilbur Whitaker, coming out of our room—"

"Coming out of your room?" Ossie interrupted. "This could be serious."

"Yes, he was coming out of our room. And when I confronted him, he made the excuse that he was looking in to see if we were taking a nap. Can you imagine, looking into our room? Anyway, I always lock the door when we're inside," Lily continued. "I was just shocked."

"We must report this to the captain, who, by the way, did not have any more information about this man than you already know," Ossie said. "Lily, you should have gone to the captain as soon as this happened."

"No, Ossie, I have a plan," Lily told him as she sipped her coffee. "I'm going to be nice to him and make like I've forgotten the incident—"

"Are you out of your mind, Lily?" Ossie interrupted, excitedly pushing his spectacles up on his nose.

"No, no, Ossie, let me explain," Lily said. "I believe he is spying on me for some reason—like a detective or something—and I can't figure out what or why, because I never saw him before. But, anyhow, if I am friendly with him I believe I can get him to talk enough to find out a few things."

"Lily, your papa would never permit this," Ossie said in a disappointed voice. "This man could be dangerous, for all we know."

"I'll only see him when there are other people around," Lily said. "That way there will be no danger of anything. I understand there's a storyteller on the ship, and I'm sure Violet will find her interesting. Could you take her to hear the storytime while I see Wilbur tomorrow?"

"Just what do you expect to find out?" Ossie asked, exasperated.

"Well, I don't know, but I'd like to know why he's so interested in me," Lily replied as she began eating.

"Lily, listen to me, you are a nice-looking young woman, and any young man in his good senses would be attracted to you—" Ossie began.

"Oh, Ossie, you are a flatterer," Lily cut him short. "Besides, I have seen plenty of other, as you say, 'nice-looking young women' on this ship, and he could probably have his pick of any, because he isn't bad-looking, you know."

"You only intend talking to him, is that right?" Ossie asked as he laid his fork down and picked up his cup of coffee.

"Well, yes, that's all," Lily looked at him in surprise. She wondered what else Ossie thought she was going to do? Allow the strange man to hold her hand or kiss her or something? "First of all, I'll accept an invitation to dine with him the next time he asks me."

"Do you really think he's going to ask you again after you caught him red-handed searching your room?" Ossie said, setting his cup back down.

Lily buttered a biscuit and replied, "He has been so insistent that I believe if I just smile at him the next time I see him, he'll begin asking again."

"If you are really going to do such a foolhardy thing you can be sure I'll keep an eye on you," Ossie told her.

By that point, Violet was finishing her food and had picked up on the conversation. She asked, "Ossie, could we walk all over this ship? Lily says it's too big. Could we, Ossie?"

"We'll walk till your legs get too tired to move anymore," Ossie promised with a smile. Turning back to Lily, he said, "I have ways to observe without being seen."

"If you say so," Lily said, finishing her food.

Violet cleaned off her plate and asked, "Ossie, I'm all done. Could we go walking now?"

Ossie looked at Lily for permission, and she said, "Go ahead. I'll wait in a chair outside on the deck."

"All right," Ossie said as everyone stood up. "Let's go, Violet."

The sun was still shining, and Lily found a chair near the dining room door in the shade. She watched Ossie and Violet walk on down the deck.

Other passengers were beginning to come outside, and Lily looked over each one. There really was an abundant supply of young females on board, and most of them were traveling in groups or with older women. She wondered why Wilbur insisted on seeing her instead of any of these others. Maybe it was because she was from Fountain Inn, where his family now lived. *Did his attention have something to do with that?* Her thoughts were suddenly interrupted.

"I say there, 'tis a lovely day, is it not?" a male voice said. Lily looked up and realized the man in the next chair was talking to her. He was an older man with grey around the temples and sharp black eyes.

Lily smiled at him. His chair was only a couple feet away, and she hoped he would not start up a conversation. "Yes, it is," she replied, and turned her attention back in the other direction.

"I say there, are you American?" the man called to her.

Lily looked at him and said, "Yes, sir, I am."

"First time for me, coming to the United States," he replied. "Can you give me an idea of what to expect in Charleston where we are going to leave this ship?"

Lily was becoming irritated. "I'm sorry, sir, I've only passed through Charleston once, and that was on my way to England. And I won't be stopping there when we dock," Lily replied.

As she said this she wondered what connections she and Violet could make to get home from Charleston. Thank goodness Ossie would be with them. He would take care of everything, since he was also going home.

Out of the corner of her eye she saw the older man rise and walk on down the deck. She also saw Ossie and Violet standing at the rail a good distance away. He was talking to Violet, but Lily could see that he was watching her instead of her little sister. She wished he wouldn't worry about her so much. She could take care of herself.

As the sun turned and part of her shade disappeared, Lily stood up to move to a cooler spot. She turned and walked away from where Ossie and Violet stood by the rail and suddenly saw Wilbur. He was standing by the next doorway talking to another man. At first she thought it was the man who had been sitting in the chair next to her, but she remembered that he had gone in the other direction. Then, as she got closer, she could see the man by Wilbur was younger than the one who had talked to her. This man was medium height and weight, dark haired, and he was wearing expensive-looking clothes.

Lily didn't want to get Wilbur's attention, so she stopped and went back the other way. She found an empty chair close to where she had been sitting and decided to sit there. A waiter nearby was serving tea and coffee from a cart.

After glancing back to see that Wilbur was still talking with his friend on the deck, she sat down and accepted a cup of coffee from the waiter. She was immediately sorry she had done this because the liquid was too hot to drink and she would just have to hold it until it cooled. If she set it on the floor next to her chair, someone might tip it over. The waiter with the cart had already moved on, so she sat with her drink and fidgeted in the chair.

Wilbur soon left the man and started walking in her direction. She didn't know whether he had seen her or not, but she turned her head so he wouldn't know she had been watching. In a few moments, he walked past her without a glance in her direction, so she assumed he had not seen her.

"Well!" she muttered to herself as she struggled with her long skirts and the cup of hot coffee. She managed to get to her feet, but the cup suddenly went flying off the saucer and landed on the deck nearby.

"Oh, my goodness!" she said in alarm. She shook her dress and examined it for coffee stains. There was only one small spot, which she rubbed away with her white glove.

She looked up and saw Wilbur standing over her. He asked, "Are you all right?" He had evidently been surprised by the coffee cup she had dropped and turned around to find her examining her dress.

"I'm fine," she said. "Thanks. The cup broke and—" She noticed the waiter had returned and now was busy picking up the pieces and mopping the floor with a cloth.

"Let me have that," Wilbur said as he took the saucer she was still holding and handed it to the waiter. "That must have been hot coffee. Are you sure you're all right?" He stepped back and looked up and down her dress.

"Oh, sure," Lily said, remembering to give him a big smile. She added, "It's so nice of you to come to my rescue."

Wilbur smiled back at her with what Lily believed to be a sincere smile. "Anytime, anywhere," he said. "Here or in Fountain Inn."

"I appreciate that," Lily replied.

"What do you say we go inside and get a fresh cup of coffee?" Wilbur asked.

"Well . . . ," Lily tried to make him think she was hesitating. "My little sister—"

"Yes, I know. She's walking with your friend," Wilbur told her. "So what other excuse can you give? Shall we go?"

"All right," Lily agreed. "But only for one cup of coffee, and that must be in a hurry or my little sister will wonder where I am."

Wilbur walked silently along with her to the small coffee shop inside and pulled out a chair for her before he spoke again.

"Now, coffee?" he asked as a waiter approached them.

"Yes, please," Lily said.

"And one for me, too," Wilbur told the man, who rushed off and came back almost instantly with a small coffeepot, two cups, and two saucers, which he placed before them.

"That was a coincidence that you came along when I needed help," Lily said with a smile as she filled their cups.

"No, it wasn't really," Wilbur said. "I saw your friend go walking with your little sister and was wondering if I could get up the nerve to approach you after that horrible blunder I made opening the door to your room. I'm really and truly sorry for that."

"Oh, forget it," Lily said. "I suppose I was overly excited about it. I was tired, and Violet was sleepy."

"Anyway, you won't have to worry about that happening again," Wilbur said, sipping his coffee and looking at her. "Who is this friend of yours? Is he from Fountain Inn?"

"Oh, yes, he is," Lily replied, holding the cup on the saucer. "He's our next-door neighbor. His name is Ossie Creighton. Have you met him?"

"No, I don't believe I have, but then it'll take a while to get acquainted with everyone," Wilbur replied.

"Ossie has been in England for several weeks on business, so he probably wasn't even home when your family moved to Fountain Inn," Lily said, watching for his reaction.

"I suppose not," Wilbur said. "Do you plan on spending all your time with him until the ship docks? I mean, is he *that* kind of friend, or just a neighbor?"

"Oh, Ossie is *just* a neighbor, as you say," Lily quickly assured him. "But he's my best friend also, like a brother." Lily continued watching his face for any response.

She noticed Wilbur did not look directly at her when he

asked, "You say he's a neighbor. You mean his property joins your father's?"

"That's right," Lily said. "Our land has been in our family since colonial days, and Ossie's land has been in his family just as long."

She finished the small cup of coffee and felt that she should leave now in order to keep Wilbur from thinking she was too interested in staying around to talk to him.

"Thanks for the coffee, but I must get Violet," she said as she rose from the table.

"The pleasure was all mine," Wilbur said as he stood up as well.

As they walked to the door and on outside, Lily spotted Ossie by the rail. "I have to go now," she told Wilbur, waving her hand in Ossie's direction.

"Are you sure you won't change your mind about having breakfast with me tomorrow?" Wilbur asked.

"Well," Lily hesitated as she looked up at him. "Not breakfast, but I could make it at noon. Ossie has promised to take Violet to hear the storyteller, and I'll be alone then."

Wilbur gave her a big smile and said, "That's just wonderful! I'll tap on your door at twelve noon."

"Oh, no, let's just meet at the door to the dining room at twelve o'clock," Lily suggested.

"See you then," Wilbur agreed. He turned and walked away.

Lily smiled to herself as she hurried toward Ossie. She could feel it—the adventure was about to begin.

Chapter Three
Ossie's Warning

W ell, did you learn anything?" Ossie asked when Lily joined him at the rail. Violet hung on the rail near them, mesmerized by the waves and swells of the sea.

"He didn't know who you were and had never heard your name. His family must have come to town after you left for England," Lily said, smiling. "But I do have another chance to ask questions. I'm meeting him at noon in the dining room tomorrow, while you and Violet are listening to the storyteller. It would be a good time to talk without Violet around to interrupt."

Ossie took his spectacles off and wiped them on a clean white handkerchief from his jacket pocket. He put them back on and cleared his throat before he finally looked at Lily. "I sure hope you're not biting off more than you can chew," he said. "You don't know what you're getting into."

"But I'm not getting into anything, really," Lily protested. "I'm only going to dine with him. If I get the right chance, I'll ask a few questions."

"Depends on what kind of questions you ask and what kind of answers you get," Ossie said. "If the man is dishonest, a crook or something, he could be dangerous if he suspects you are getting too inquisitive. Remember that."

"I won't do anything to make him suspicious," Lily said. She wouldn't admit it to Ossie, but his warning did make her feel a little frightened, especially when she thought of how she had caught Wilbur coming out of her room. But on the ship she was always around other people, and she would remember to keep her door locked when she was in her room.

"Remember, Lily, I have watched you grow up, and I know you have never been exposed to law-breaking people," Ossie said. "I judge this man to be a law-breaker. And you just don't realize how ruthless and dangerous men like that can be. Nothing matters to such people except their own, personal desires—which they will achieve without any thought for anyone else."

Lily leaned against the rail beside Ossie as she thought about his words. Even if Wilbur were dangerous, she still believed she could safely get information as to who he really was and what he was after. She couldn't imagine what there was about her or the things in her room that Wilbur could possibly be interested in.

"I'll keep you posted as to what I'm doing," Lily promised as she straightened up to look into Ossie's serious brown eyes.

Ossie smoothed back his dark brown hair as the wind ruffled it and replied, "Make sure you do that. Without your father around to advise you, I feel responsible to see that you get home all right."

Lily's thoughts flew back to the reason they were going home. "Ossie, did you see my father right before you left for England? Was he all right?" she asked, holding on to her long skirts as the strong gusts blew off the waves and swished about her legs.

"Yes, in fact, I went over the day I left to tell him I would be gone. I wanted him to know where I was in case anything came up requiring special attention on my farm. The men I have hired are all good workers and I trust them, but I asked the foreman to see your father if anything unexpected happened," Ossie explained. "And your father certainly wasn't sick then. He was shoeing the judge's horse and had three more lined up to replace shoes."

"Maybe he's not ill at all," Lily said wishfully. "Since the message was signed by someone we don't know, maybe it was all a hoax."

"But, Lily, why would someone send you the fare to come home if it was not necessary?" Ossie reminded her.

"I just don't know what to think. This ship is so slow and this is all so disquieting to live with until I do reach home," Lily said, frowning and staring into space.

"You know how busy your father has been since your mother died," Ossie said. "He never seems to stop work whether he's shoeing horses or working the fields."

"I know, Ossie," Lily said. "We need the money. We've got bills piled up from my mother's illness over the last few years. I need to find some way to make money and help out, but instead of letting me try to find work he sent me and Violet to Aunt Emma's in England so he could try to catch up."

Ossie cleared his throat, adjusted his spectacles, and said, "There's a possibility Mr. Dutton might could use help in his office where I work."

"But I wouldn't know anything about office work," Lily said. "I know how to sew just about anything, and I think I'm pretty good at it. But I'd have to have customers, and all the people I know do their own sewing."

"Have you thought about getting married? You *are* sixteen now," Ossie said hesitantly.

"Oh, Ossie, Papa has never even allowed me to keep company with young men. He's always said I was too young, and then when I finally reached sixteen in July, my mother died and Papa sent us off to England," Lily said in a rush.

"Well, now that you are sixteen, I'm sure your father will give you more rope," Ossie said.

"I don't think I would want to be dependent on a man," Lily said. "I'd like to get out and fend for myself. Besides, I'd feel like I was accepting charity to get married just for a livelihood."

"Oh, no. Never, never get married for that reason. Love must come first, ahead of everything else. If two people don't sincerely love each other, then a marriage would never work out. I didn't mean that you should get married in order to have someone support you. What I meant was . . . surely a young, pretty girl like you must have lots of admirers, and you must have had some interest in someone," Ossie quickly explained.

Lily looked at him, puzzled at all this advice. She couldn't remember any boy that she would have been interested in for more than normal friendship. And she had had lots of friends while growing up in school and at church.

"Ossie, I have to say, I have never met a boy I would be interested in marrying. Now, let's change the subject," she said, smiling slightly. "How about you? I know you loved your wife, but she has been dead over ten years, Ossie, and I've never known you to even look at another woman. You are still young and you are all alone. Why haven't you got yourself another wife?"

Ossie's face turned red and he dropped his gaze. "That's a different story," he said. "Once you find true love, it's impossible to replace it."

Lily shivered and suddenly realized the air was cooling as the sun disappeared beneath the horizon.

"I think we'd better go inside with Violet," she suggested.

"Let's go in now, Violet," called Ossie.

She looked up and started excitedly telling Lily what she had seen on her walk with Ossie. But food was always the first thing on her mind, and as they passed the coffee room she asked, "Could we get hot chocolate?"

"Sounds good to me," Lily replied.

"And me," Ossie added.

"I hope they have cookies to go with it," Violet said, skipping ahead as Lily and Ossie followed her toward the door.

Once inside the coffee room, Ossie led them to a table. They sat down and a waiter brought them hot chocolate, and Violet got her cookies, which occupied her attention.

Lily looked across the room and saw the man who had been in the chair beside her earlier that afternoon. He was drinking coffee with another man who had his back toward her. While she watched them, the other man turned his head slightly and she was surprised to see he was the man Wilbur had been talking to on deck. These two seemed to know each other, for they laughed together and had a lively discussion, which Lily couldn't understand from her table.

"Do you know those people?" Ossie asked, noticing Lily's attention focused on the two.

"Not really," Lily replied. "But I saw them both out on the deck this afternoon, and the older one tried to talk to me."

"Evidently both of these men know Wilbur Whitaker," Ossie surmised as he glanced at the men.

"Well, I'm positive the younger one does, because he was talking to Wilbur today. But I'm not sure about the other one," Lily said. "However, it is a big coincidence that the two should be such good buddies, and that the older one tried to begin a conversation with me on the deck."

"That question is about to be answered," Ossie said. "Here comes Wilbur."

Lily saw him enter the room. Avoiding eye contact with him, she watched as he walked over to the two men. He did seem to be acquainted with the older man, for they exchanged friendly greetings and Wilbur sat down next to him.

"Well!" Lily exclaimed softly to Ossie. "The mystery deepens."

"And that puts you against three men in any attempt to get information," Ossie reminded her.

Lily thought for a moment and then said, "Anyhow, I'll keep my appointment with Wilbur at noon tomorrow."

And she did, in spite of Ossie's warnings. Wilbur was already waiting at the doorway to the dining room when she arrived at two minutes till twelve. She had not arrived too early to make him think she was overly anxious for his company.

Ossie was in charge of Violet and they were eating in a snack room at the end of the deck before they went to listen to the storyteller.

Wilbur was leaning on the wall next to the doorway, and Lily thought the expression on his face was one of anger. He frowned and squinted into the distance, unaware that she was looking at him. But the minute she spoke, the angry look turned to charm.

"I made it," she said, for want of anything else to say. She wondered what he had been thinking about.

"And I am delighted. Let's go inside," Wilbur said with a big smile as he opened the door for her.

They both remained silent until they had been seated and the food had arrived. Even then Lily could sense Wilbur's reluctance to talk. He was a strange man.

"My friend Ossie has taken Violet to hear a storyteller," Lily said, trying to make conversation.

"That's nice," Wilbur said, slicing the ham on his plate.

Lily buttered her biscuit and thought for a few moments before she asked, "Are you going home to Fountain Inn as soon as we dock in Charleston?"

Wilbur looked up, a puzzled frown on his face, and answered, "It all depends on some business I will be transacting in Charleston." He sipped the coffee from his cup.

"Violet and I will be getting the first train out of Charleston," Lily said. "I'm in a hurry to get home to see about my father."

Wilbur coughed and almost choked on the coffee before he set the cup down. Holding a napkin in front of his face, he coughed again. "I'm sorry," he finally managed to say.

"Maybe if you drink some water . . . ," Lily suggested as she motioned to the glass of water standing by his plate.

But instead of drinking the water, Wilbur lifted the coffee cup and drank its contents in one big gulp. Then he touched the napkin to his mouth and cleared his throat. "I'm truly sorry," he said. "I'm not very good at talking and drinking at the same time." He cleared his throat again and finally smiled.

Lily smiled back at him and said, "Neither am I, but I've learned there's a trick to it. You don't take a breath to speak while the fluid is going down."

Wilbur thought for a moment and said, "You're right. I'll try to remember that next time." He dug into the mashed potatoes on his plate.

"So you do work for your father then?" Lily asked as she began eating the buttered biscuit.

"Work for my father? Oh, you mean because of what I said about doing business in Charleston? Well, a little now and then," Wilbur said.

"What kind of business is your father in?" Lily asked without looking at him, trying to seem nonchalant about the question.

"Business? Oh, my father is involved in lots of business deals," he said.

Lily tried to figure out what she could ask to get more information. "What kind of business does he own in Charleston?" she asked, still not looking directly at him.

"He doesn't *own* a business in Charleston. He only has contacts there," Wilbur said. Then laying down his fork for a moment, he added, "I'd much rather talk about you than my father."

Lily felt her face turn red, but she was sure he wasn't sincere about that. He seemed to have two personalities: one charming and the other ruthless. Evidently he was using his charm to try to get information from her. *But what for?* she wondered. *Why is he interested in anything I do or anything I have?*

"There's not much about me to discuss," Lily said, finally looking directly at him. "My father is a blacksmith and we are only poor working people, not wealthy like your family with all these business doings."

Wilbur coughed again and looked off to the side before he replied, "Which makes you more interesting and uncomplicated."

"I doubt that," Lily said, smiling at him. "Aunt Ida May says I lead a very complicated life."

"And who is Aunt Ida May?" Wilbur asked. "And why does she have such an opinion of you?"

"Aunt Ida May is my father's spinster sister. She lives with Aunt Janie Belle and her husband, Uncle Aaron Woods," Lily explained. "Aunt Ida May always says I don't lead the life of a normal young lady."

"You don't?" Wilbur asked in surprise. "Why not?"

"I've been taking care of Violet ever since she was born six years ago. My mother became an invalid then, and I also had to nurse her during her illness. I am also housekeeper for my father," Lily explained, and then added, "Oh, I am also the family seamstress."

"Whew!" Wilbur exclaimed. "When do you have time to be just a young lady with an opportunity for social doings?"

"I don't so far," Lily said. "You see, I just turned sixteen back in July and I have not had a chance to do any of those frivolous things young ladies do, like go to socials or hayrides or church outings and so forth."

"I think it's about time you caught up with life then," Wilbur told her. He leaned across the table to smile at her. "Would you have time for me to come calling after we get home?"

Lily felt flustered. This conversation was not taking the right course. He was interrogating her. It would have to be the other way around if she was ever to learn anything about him. She didn't look directly at him and hesitated about replying to his question.

"May I?" Wilbur insisted. He reached his hand across the table toward her hands.

Lily quickly put her hands in her lap and glanced at him, then looked across the room. She uttered the first answer she could think of. "I would have to ask Papa," she said.

Wilbur straightened up and looked at her with a frown. "Why do you have to ask your father? You said you're sixteen years old."

Then it dawned on Lily that he was from up north, where folks probably had a different set of rules for young ladies. "Because we live in the south, and that's the way things are done," she said.

"That's a strange way to live," he said. "What happens if a young lady does not have any parents to ask permission from?"

"Oh, well, there's always a relative who is responsible for the upbringing of a young person, boy or girl," Lily explained. "And if there isn't a relative, there's always a close friend of the family."

"Whatever the rules are, I'd like to see you after we get home. We'll just have to arrange it somehow, that is, if you are interested," Wilbur told her.

"I don't know, Wilbur," Lily replied, frowning. "I don't really know you or anything about you, and I've just met you here on the ship."

"Well, we can remedy that. We can become better acquainted during the rest of our journey," he said with a big smile.

He is handsome, Lily thought as he spoke. *He can be so nice when he wants to, but there is another side to him. He is probably not very honest, because I think he lied his way out of the reason for going into my room. But I still have to make him think I'm interested if I am to learn anything about him.*

She looked at him with a slight smile and said, "Maybe."

"All right," he said, leaning back and smiling at her.

"But please understand, I am in charge of my little sister and I have to put her ahead of my pleasures," Lily reminded him. "That means I have little time to call my own." She didn't want him to think he could tie up all her time.

"I understand," Wilbur said, his smile vanishing. "I have some business to attend to here aboard ship, so we'll just work in whatever time we can. All right?"

Lily thought he must be talking about the two men she had seen him with. Maybe they had something to do with his father's business. It was strange, though, that the older man had tried to start a conversation with her.

"We'll see," Lily replied. They were both finished eating, so she said, "I need to find Violet and Ossie now." She pushed back in her chair.

Wilbur immediately stood up, came over, and held the chair for her to rise. They walked to the doorway, where Lily paused and said, "Thank you for asking me to dine with you. I enjoyed it."

"So did I, and I look forward to more chances to get to know you." Wilbur pushed open the door and they stepped out onto the deck.

Lily spotted Violet and Ossie walking along the deck. After telling Wilbur a quick "good-bye," she hurried to catch them.

"Oh, this is a big ship! The story lady told us that it is big enough to hold hundreds of people," Violet exclaimed.

"It certainly is big," Lily agreed. Turning to Ossie, she asked, "Did Violet wear you out?"

"Oh, no, the storyteller spun a marvelous tale. Afterward we walked around the whole ship, but I've enjoyed showing Violet around. She's a bright little girl," Ossie said with a smile. "She'll probably graduate from school before she's sixteen years old, just like her sister did."

"Without your help in math I'd never have made it," Lily replied.

"But you can't be good in everything," Ossie said.

Lily noticed that Violet was listening to the conversation. So she quickly added to Ossie's remark, "But you should try." She looked down at her sister and smiled.

The child frowned and didn't say a word, but she looked thoughtful.

"Let's sit down somewhere," Ossie suggested. He looked around the deck and spotted three empty chairs a short distance away. "There," he said and pointed to the seats.

But Violet objected to sitting on the deck. She wanted to go hear more from the storyteller, so Ossie took her into the reading room while Lily held the chairs for the two of them.

Lily looked around the deck for Wilbur. She had not noticed where he went after she joined Ossie. Now he was nowhere in sight.

Ossie came back to join Lily and said, "It does feel good to sit down. And did you make any progress?"

"Not much," Lily replied. "He will be transacting business in Charleston for his father. He would like to come calling at home—"

"You didn't agree, I hope," Ossie interrupted.

"I have to ask Papa," Lily said. "He would like to become better acquainted on the ship. I told him I didn't have much time because I have to care for Violet. Besides, he has business to attend to on shipboard. But we may have a chance for some time together."

Ossie frowned at Lily and said, "Why do you want to do this? I see no reason for it."

"I believe now that he may have the same idea I have, that is, to get all the information about me that he can while I'm trying to find out things about him. He certainly did ask a lot of questions," Lily explained. "But he didn't get any answers that I didn't want to give."

"I can only hope you won't get involved in something you'll be sorry for," Ossie said with an exasperated sigh.

They talked the afternoon away. Finally Lily said she should go get Violet.

As they stood up, Ossie asked, "Are you dining with Violet and me tonight, or with that man?"

Lily laughed. "Of course I'm dining with you and Violet tonight if you'll allow me," she said.

"Shall I meet you two at the dining room door at roundabout six o'clock?" Ossie asked.

"Fine," Lily replied. They walked to the door, and Ossie held it open for her as she asked, "Which direction is your room?"

"I suppose you'd say I'm on the other side of the ship," Ossie explained. He pointed down the corridor. "I have to go that way. See you at six," he said before he walked on.

When Lily picked up Violet, she was full of tales about Little Red Riding Hood and continued to talk about the story until they got to their room.

Before Lily even touched the door handle, she realized the door was not completely shut. She paused to look at it and then slowly pushed the door open. Violet rushed ahead of her.

There was no place for anyone to hide except in the tiny closet. Lily slid the closet door open and looked inside, where she found nothing but their clothes hanging. She pushed the door shut.

"All right, let's just rest awhile before supper," Lily told Violet. "You get your book and read while I write in my journal." Violet took her book and climbed up into her bunk.

Lily realized she had forgotten to lock their door. She rushed across the room and slid the inside latch closed. She took her journal and a pencil from her bag and sat on her bed.

She looked curiously down at the notebook in her hand. "Has someone been in here reading my journal? I've been leaving it right there in that bag where they could easily find it," she murmured to herself.

"They wouldn't find anything of interest," she reminded herself. Lily had not been writing anything personal in the journal. It was more or less just a record of happenings each day.

She looked around the small cabin, wondering what someone might be searching for. When she and Violet had boarded the ship, Lily had unpacked enough clothes for the journey and hung them in the little closet. The rest of their belongings were in the two trunks sitting in the corner, and she had kept these locked. She carried the keys on the chain to her locket, which she pushed beneath the front of her dress.

Their few toiletries were on the vanity table. And there was nothing else for anyone to search.

The lock on their door had been broken when they moved into the cabin, and promises were made to repair it. Even though she had asked about it several times, nothing had been done. The latest word was that a part was needed and this piece would not be available until they docked. In the meantime one of the crewmen had worked on the inside latch and fixed it. But when Lily and Violet were out of their room, anyone could open the door and come in.

The more Lily thought about it, the more she thought maybe she had not securely closed the door when they had left the cabin. She had been in a rush to meet Wilbur at the dining room.

But now she wanted to write an entry in her journal. And when she was finished she would lock it up in her trunk.

Chapter Four
Tragedy at Sea!

A s soon as they had settled down at the supper table, Lily told Ossie about her door.

"The door was not closed all the way when Violet and I went back after I talked to you," Lily explained. "I'm not sure I shut it tight when we left earlier but I thought I had."

Ossie asked, "Anything missing? Or disturbed?"

"No, not that I could see," she replied. "So maybe I did leave it partly open. I suppose I'm just overly sensitive about things like that after finding Wilbur coming out of our room."

"You need to keep an eye out for him," Ossie said. "You don't really know the man."

Lily was becoming irritated with Ossie's remarks about Wilbur. She appreciated Ossie's concern, but he was repeating his cautionary remarks. She was old enough to know how to take care of herself, so she didn't reply to his statement, but kept right on eating.

"Do you have plans for when you get back home? Now that Violet will be going to school you'll have more time for yourself," Ossie said, changing the subject as though he sensed her attitude.

"I suppose I'll just be lost without my mother to nurse and without Violet home all day. I'm hoping I can find some way to help my father with his finances," Lily said sadly as she thought of her mother's long years of suffering.

"As I mentioned before, you might find something to do in Mr. Dutton's office. I know you don't have any experience in office work, but you can always learn," Ossie reminded her, sipping his coffee. "You could approach Mr. Dutton with the offer of working for very little pay in order to get some experience."

"Thanks for the suggestion, Ossie. I'll think about it," Lily replied, and she put another biscuit on the plate Violet was holding out toward her.

"Potatoes, too," Violet told her, still holding out her plate.

Lily spooned more mashed potatoes onto it. Then she looked at Ossie and said, "I wonder if Wilbur's father has opened a business in Fountain Inn."

"He might have, but you don't know what kind of business he's in, do you?" Ossie asked.

"Wilbur won't give any actual facts. He just said his family had so much money he didn't have to work," Lily replied. "But I intend finding out more about him and his family." She looked around the dining room and said, "I don't see him in here tonight."

"Since this place almost never closes, he has plenty of time to come and eat without you ever seeing him," Ossie said.

"I agreed I would see him again when I have time and when he has time," she explained. "He said he has business to attend to while we're on the ship and I would imagine that involves those two men we saw him talking to last night."

"There's bound to be something not just right about a man's business if he won't talk about it," Ossie said while he sipped his coffee. "An honest man is willing to discuss his achievements and how he arrived where he is in his career."

"I agree on that, Ossie," she said before swallowing a mouthful of stewed squash. "I think there's something wrong and I just want to find out what it is and why he is interested in me."

The ship suddenly lurched, causing dishes to slide about on their table. Lily grabbed at things to keep them from falling to the floor. Violet held so tightly to the tablecloth she almost pulled it off. Ossie quickly pushed back his chair and stood up, steadying himself as the ship lurched again.

"What is happening?" Violet exclaimed in fright. She could hear the giant engine working hard and the ship seemed to slow in the water.

"I don't know, but we'll find out," Ossie said as he started toward the door of the dining room, followed by most of the diners in the room.

"Wait!" Lily called to him. She quickly helped Violet down from her chair, grasped her firmly by the hand, and hurried after Ossie.

There were already people outside on the deck, and the crowd from the dining room made it hard to move.

Ossie looked around and asked the crowd, "What's happened?"

A crewman making his way through the crowd called back to him, "Man overboard! We've reversed the engines to stop." He disappeared toward the rail.

"Somebody is in the water!" Lily gasped.

Ossie continued pushing ahead, while Lily held on to his coattail and pulled Violet along by the hand. Here and there people moved back a little to allow them through. The other passengers seemed to have halted to await further action from the crew.

Finally Lily could see the rail and noticed probably a dozen crewmen there as they lowered a lifeboat with several of the men in it. She tried to see over them and into the water, but she was not able to get close enough.

Ossie, by her side, reached to put his arm around her as he said, "You should take Violet and move back some. This may not be pleasant to see."

Lily then felt the impact of the whole situation. Some poor fellow was down in the water, probably struggling for his life. "Oh, dear God, please help them to save him," she whispered as she squeezed Violet close to her skirts.

Violet looked up at her with eyes full of excitement and asked, "How did the man get in the water?"

"We don't know, dear," Lily told her as she moved through an opening in the crowd to stand at the wall of the deck. She could still see enough from here and Violet would be protected from seeing anything bad. Ossie had stayed where he was.

Suddenly the ship's horn blasted the air. Lily jumped and held Violet close. She looked around for explanation, and an older man had noticed her and volunteered to explain, "We have to let other ships know we are standing here right in their paths. And you see the light up there?"

Lily looked up and realized she had not previously noticed the moving light above. It was not yet dark, but it was foggy. The light made a swoop down in the direction where the crew was working. She could see men bringing the lifeboat up. As soon as it was level with the deck, the crewmen in it jumped out and pulled a man onto the deck. They worked with him for a few minutes and then stood up, shaking their heads.

"Oh, no!" Lily whispered to herself.

She saw Ossie making his way through the crowd toward her. His head was slightly bowed, and when he straightened up to look at her she knew the man had died.

"Too late?" she questioned when he got to her side.

"Yes, too late, and do you know who it is?" Ossie asked, removing his spectacles so he could wipe them with the white handkerchief from his pocket.

"No, I couldn't tell from here. Is it—someone I know?" Lily asked, her heart pounding.

"Not really," Ossie said as he put his glasses back on and looked at her. "It was the older man whom we saw Wilbur talking to."

"Oh, I'm so sorry," Lily said sadly. "And he never even got to the United States."

Ossie looked at her questioningly.

"He told me this was his first trip to the United States when he tried to talk to me yesterday afternoon," Lily explained. "What happened?"

"They don't know yet, but the man seemed to be badly beaten, and my guess is that couldn't have happened just by jumping or falling overboard," Ossie replied. "Let's go back inside and get coffee."

"Yes, we left our food, but I was finished anyway," Lily said as the three turned back to the door.

"Me, too, except for the chocolate cake," Violet said as she jerked Lily's hand and looked up at her.

"All right, we'll have chocolate cake," Lily agreed.

There was a steady buzz everywhere as the passengers discussed what had happened. A lot of the other people returned to the dining room, too, but Lily and Ossie found their table untouched, just the way they had left it.

"I just can't imagine what happened to the man," Lily said. She shivered as she thought about it. Ossie reached to hold her hand.

"I would say the man had been in a fight and lost," Ossie said. "I didn't see your friend Wilbur in the crowd."

"Not my *friend*, Ossie, just Wilbur," Lily corrected him and withdrew her hand. "No, and when I think about it, I didn't see him either."

The ship trembled as it began moving forward again.

"I suppose they are finished searching the water," Ossie said.

"Searching the water?" Lily asked. "What could they find in the water?"

"Oh, lots of things. Maybe an instrument used to strike the man, or maybe another man, or whatever," Ossie replied. "I'm sure since the man was already dead they did a search."

"I hope they found something to explain why the man was overboard," Lily said.

Ossie reached again for Lily's hand and held it as he said, "Look at me, Lily, and listen well. I believe Wilbur Whitaker is a dangerous man, especially now with this friend of his apparently killed. You've got to stay away from him."

Lily looked into Ossie's serious brown eyes. It all came home to her at once. Wilbur probably was dangerous, and she knew she could not talk to him anymore. "You're right, Ossie," she said. "I'll avoid him from now on."

46

"Well, thank goodness you've come to your senses," Ossie said, still holding her hand. He gave it a squeeze.

"I'd still like to know why he's so interested in me, but I'll just wait till I get home to Papa and pursue that," Lily told him. "But, of course, I may never see him again once we get home. His family is so wealthy that we won't be moving in the same circles, and I won't be going to the same places as he does."

"That's good. I hope you never see him again," Ossie said. "And until we dock in Charleston, I'll be right at your side to keep you away from him."

Lily smiled and looked up at him. "Oh, Ossie, I don't need a bodyguard."

"Never mind that," he said. "I plan to stick to you like molasses so I can be sure you're safe. I know your papa would want me to do that."

"Oh, yes. To Papa I'm still his little girl," Lily said with a smile. But then she frowned as she asked, "Ossie, do you think Wilbur was involved in this man's death?"

"I don't know, Lily, but I do know they knew each other." Ossie released her hand and picked up his coffee cup. "I suppose the ship's captain will begin an investigation, and we may learn something from that."

"I wonder where the other fellow is, the young one who was talking to Wilbur earlier," Lily said thoughtfully. "I hope the captain knows that Wilbur and this other fellow knew the one who went overboard."

"I'll see that he does," Ossie promised. "I'll talk to the captain tomorrow morning."

Lily was still thinking about the man that night when she went to bed. She wondered whether he was honest or whether he was involved in unsavory doings. She was sure now that Wilbur was hiding something, but exactly what she had no idea. And if the dead man had been his friend, had he also been involved in whatever it was Wilbur was doing? On the other hand, she asked herself if the man found out whatever Wilbur was covering up and told him he would not go along with that. Would Wilbur have beaten him up and thrown him overboard?

"I do hope Ossie gets to talk to the captain in the morning," she murmured to herself.

Then her thoughts turned toward home. What was ailing her father? Would he be recovered by the time they got home? And, most of all, did he even know someone had sent for her and Violet to come home? He had been firm about sending them both to stay with Aunt Emma in England until he had straightened out his finances.

"Oh, Papa, I love you," Lily whispered to herself.

The night seemed long. Lily kept dozing off and then waking up. Finally Violet slid down from her upper bunk, and Lily knew it was time to get up. She could almost set the clock by Violet's sleeping habits.

Lily sat up on the edge of her bunk and Violet, standing before her, rubbed her eyes and asked, "Did you hear the noise next door, way in the night?"

Noise next door? She had not heard a thing. "No, Violet, I didn't," she replied. She stood up, too, and said, "Maybe you had a dream."

"No, no, Lily," Violet protested. "It was in the squinty-eyed man's room. I heard him dragging things around and going bumpity-bump. He woke me up."

Lily frowned, considering seriously what Violet was saying. Had there really been a disturbance that she hadn't heard, or had Violet dreamed it after the experience with the man overboard?

"All right," she said. "Let's get dressed. We're supposed to meet Ossie for breakfast. We'll tell him all about it." She took a fresh dress from the tiny closet and helped Violet slide into it.

As Lily picked up the hairbrush on the vanity table, Violet reached for it and said, "Lily, I want to brush my own hair. I'm old enough now."

Lily smiled, gave her the brush, and watched as she did a pretty good job of removing the tangles in her long blonde hair. Then Lily quickly got dressed herself. She also put on a fresh dress, one of her favorites that she had made while staying at Aunt Emma's, a full-skirted red gingham with pockets with a small matching scarf around the neck. She needed the boost to her sagging confidence. Wilbur's actions had proved to be a test of her skills in analyzing a situation.

Ossie's opinions had always been important to her as he hovered over her like a big brother while she was growing up. Now that she was sixteen and was expected to make her own decisions, she knew she should still listen to him. He was older and knew more about human nature than she did.

"I'm hungry," Violet protested. She watched Lily standing before the mirror, pinning up her thick blonde hair.

Lily's fingers moved faster with the hairpins and she turned to Violet, smiling. "So am I. Let's go," she replied.

They arrived at the dining room and found Ossie, as always, on time and dependable. After greeting the two sisters, he led the way into the dining room to a table.

"Ossie, somebody was banging things around last night in the squinty-eyed man's room," Violet told him. Meanwhile, Lily began filling her sister's plate.

Ossie looked surprised and asked, "Did you get to see what they were doing?" He glanced at Lily.

"No, no. I was asleep," Violet said as Lily placed the plate before her. She ignored any more conversation as she dug into the food.

Lily said in an undertone, "I'm not sure whether she dreamed it or she really did hear something. I didn't hear it myself, and I was awake off and on for the whole night."

"Shall we go look after we eat?" Ossie asked.

"You mean look in Wilbur's room?" Lily asked in surprise.

"Why not?" Ossie said. "If there was really enough noise to disturb your sister who knows what might have been going on in that room?"

"Suppose he catches us? After all, I let him know I didn't like it when I caught him coming out of my room," Lily said as she buttered a biscuit.

"We won't let him catch us," Ossie said. "If we're careful he'll never know it."

"If you say so," Lily agreed reluctantly.

"Breakfast time will be over by then, so I should be able to catch the captain to talk to him about Wilbur and his friends," Ossie told her as he sliced the ham on his plate.

"Ossie, you keep warning me to stay out of things," Lily said with a laugh, "but you keep doing detective work yourself."

"That's only to keep you from getting involved in something over your head," Ossie replied with a grin.

Lily looked at him mischievously and said, "Yes, I know."

When the three had finished their morning meal and prepared to leave the table, Violet jumped down from her chair and said, "Now are we ready to go look in Wilbur's room?"

Lily and Ossie looked at each other and burst into laughter. Evidently the child had not been completely absorbed in her food, for she had understood the point of what they were talking about the whole time.

"Sh-h-h!" Lily bent to hush her before she said something else that diners nearby might hear. "It's a secret. Now let's go."

"We've got a secret!" Violet gleefully said as she skipped along by her sister's side.

"Violet, now you have to be quiet about this. We don't want anyone else to know our secret or it won't be a secret," Lily warned her as they reached the dining room door.

"I won't tell," Violet whispered loudly as they went outside.

Ossie stooped down to look directly into her excited blue eyes. "In order for us to keep this a secret we have to be very quiet or we won't be able to go look in that man's room. Do you understand?"

"All right, I will be pokey and quiet. 'Sides I want to see what the squinty-eyed man has in his room," Violet said in a low voice.

"Don't forget now," Ossie cautioned her as he stood up and they continued on their way.

When they arrived in the corridor to their room and to Wilbur's room, there was no one about. Ossie motioned for Lily and Violet to stop at the corner.

"We'll just tap on the door. If he answers, we'll say we didn't see him at breakfast or something. You should do the talking," Ossie planned. "And if there is no answer, then I will open his door if it isn't locked. You and Violet stay in the hallway and warn me if you see anyone coming. I'll look around inside as fast as I can."

"All right, Ossie," Lily agreed.

The three quietly stopped before Wilbur's door. Ossie knocked. There was no answer. He knocked again. Still no answer. He tried the handle. It was unlocked. He slowly opened the door to peep in.

Lily stayed right behind him with her hand firmly grasping Violet's. She could see inside the room as Ossie finally swung the door wide open. No one was inside and the room was empty of any luggage or personal belongings. The closet, like the one in her room, stood open, but there was nothing inside.

"He's moved out!" Lily said in surprise as Ossie stepped inside and she followed.

"Yes, but where has he gone?" Ossie wondered aloud, walking around the empty room. "Not a scrap of anything left."

"Then Violet was right. There must have been some noise in here last night," Lily said.

"I told you I didn't dream it," Violet said, looking up at her.

"Yes, you probably did hear something," Ossie agreed.

As they left the room, Lily laid her hand on Ossie's arm to stop him. "You know I don't know that he ever occupied this room," she said thoughtfully. "He said he had the room next door, but I don't remember ever seeing him go in or out of this room."

Ossie frowned and pushed his spectacles up on his nose. "I don't know why he would lie about it, but you may be right," he said as they stood in the corridor.

"I suppose if he would lie about one thing, he could be completely involved in fabricating other so-called facts," Lily said. "Maybe Wilbur Whitaker is not even his name."

"No, he told the truth about that. The captain has him listed by that name," Ossie said. "Let's go out onto the deck and find chairs for you and Violet while I look for the captain."

They walked down the corridor and Lily asked, "Shouldn't I go with you to see the captain so I can tell him what I know about Wilbur?"

"No, I can relate to him everything you've told me," Ossie said. "I think the captain would be more prone to discuss the man if I go alone. If he wants to see you, then we can arrange that later."

Lily knew Ossie well enough to know that he liked to protect her from anything and everything, so she didn't say any more.

The sun was shining brightly from a cloudless sky and the air already felt warm for September. Ossie found chairs for them in the shade on the deck, away from the area where the man had been brought up from the water the day before.

"Please don't be gone too long," Lily told him. "I'll just die of curiosity."

Ossie laughed and said, "Well, I don't want you dying, so I'll be back shortly."

Lily watched as he walked down the deck toward an inside door. She had brought Violet's book in her bag and pulled it out now to give it to her.

"I thought you might want to look at this," Lily said, smiling as her little sister eagerly took it and curled up in her chair.

Lily carefully watched the passengers on the first-class deck in an effort to see if Wilbur or his friend would appear, but she saw neither one. Pretty young girls, with parasols open against the sun, paraded about while nicely dressed young men gathered in clusters, laughing and talking. She watched as one of the girls deliberately dropped a handkerchief in front of a young man as she walked past. Then Lily laughed to herself as the fellow observed the handkerchief and purposely ignored it. She was sure the girl's face must have turned red with embarrassment as she hurried to join her friends further down the deck.

Lily, inexperienced with international travel, had more or less kept to herself and looked after Violet during the journey. She had not made any friends other than Wilbur because she was too worried about her father to socialize. She constantly hoped and prayed she would find him well when they arrived home.

"Coffee, miss?" a man asked, and Lily looked up to see the same waiter who had been there when she had spilled her coffee yesterday. He was smiling and was holding two cups on a large tray.

"Well, I suppose so," Lily said, straightening up in her chair.

"Hot chocolate!" Violet immediately told him with a big grin as she closed her book.

"It's rather risky to have hot chocolate out here on the deck," Lily said.

"I will cool the chocolate and the coffee with water from the pitcher here," the waiter informed her, reaching for it on the cart behind him. "And I will place this tray on the floor by your chair for you to set it on."

"Thank you," Lily said as he arranged everything for her.

"And here is a large napkin just in case the ship shakes the hot chocolate and causes it to spill out of the young lady's cup," he told Violet. He placed the napkin on her lap and handed her the cup.

"Thank you," Violet said. "I'll be careful, but I'm not sure the ship will be."

The waiter smiled at her and moved on down the deck with his cart.

Lily sipped the coffee and found it just right, not too hot and not too cold. Violet carefully held her cup with both hands while she drank it. Ossie had still not returned by the time they finished their drinks and Lily set the cups on the tray the waiter had provided.

Violet picked up her book and looked at Lily. "I heard Ossie say I had to go to school when we get home," she began. "Do I really have to, Lily?"

"Why, yes," Lily replied. "You want to learn how to read and write, don't you? And you have to go to school in order to be able to do that."

"Well, maybe I could go just long enough to learn how to

read a book and write a little," the child agreed reluctantly. "But, you know, Lily, I can read this book already, and I *can* write my name."

Lily laughed and said, "That's because you have the book memorized, and I taught you how to write your name."

"Couldn't you just teach me whatever else I need to learn so I wouldn't have to go to school?" Violet asked.

Lily laughed again and said, "That would take forever, because I'm not a schoolteacher. You'll learn much faster if you go to school. Besides, you'll also learn a lot of other things, like drawing pictures and singing."

"But I know how to do that already," Violet reminded her.

"You'll learn to do them much better at school," Lily said. "I had to go to school. Everyone has to in order to learn all the important things in life."

"Will Ossie help me with my math, whatever that is that you said he helped you with?" Violet asked.

Lily realized Violet overheard and remembered almost everything they said. "Why, I suppose he will when you get old enough to learn math," Lily promised her. "And I see Ossie coming down the deck right now."

Ossie came up to them and pulled a nearby chair over to sit down. He looked excited, and Lily anxiously waited to hear what he had to say.

"I was able to talk with the captain," he began. He pushed his spectacles up on his nose and continued, "He wants to talk to you. It seems that Wilbur never occupied that room next door to you. The man they pulled out of the water was the passenger listed for that room."

"Really?" Lily was surprised. "Well, where did Wilbur stay? And who was that man?"

"That man's name was Milford Ibson and he was from a little town near London, England," Ossie explained. He looked at Violet and added, "That noise Violet heard during the night was evidently the crew moving Mr. Ibson's belongings out of the room. That's why it's empty now."

"And Wilbur?" Lily asked.

"Wilbur Whitaker has accommodations in the first-class section of the ship," Ossie explained.

"Then what was he doing in the second-class section where we stay?" Lily asked.

"The captain was puzzled by his actions. That's why he wants to talk to you," Ossie said.

"You asked the captain before about Wilbur, and he told you he didn't know anything about him except that he was registered, didn't you?" Lily reminded him.

"Yes, he still doesn't know anything more about the man, but he is interested in talking to you about him because he was evidently a friend of the deceased man," Ossie explained. "And as far as the other friend of Wilbur's is concerned, the younger man we've seen him with, the captain does not know whom we're talking about without a name."

"What did the captain have to say about the man who died, Mr. Ibson?" Lily asked.

"They don't know yet what happened, but there just happen to be two lawmen from the United States on board this ship, and the captain has asked them to investigate," Ossie explained.

"What did they do with the dead man?" Violet asked anxiously.

Lily immediately regretted having exposed her little sister to such sordid events. She looked at Ossie, hoping he would be gracious.

"They'll be sending him home on another ship so he can be buried in his family's graveyard. You know, like the one we have back home," Ossie explained. Turning back to Lily, he asked, "Now, when do you want to make an appointment with the captain? He said he would meet at your convenience, so anytime you wish will be all right with him."

"I suppose the sooner the better, to get it over with," Lily replied.

"Shall I go back and ask if he'll see you in, say, a half hour or so?" Ossie asked.

"That would be fine," Lily agreed. "Thank you, Ossie. I hope you'll be going with me."

Ossie stood up and said, "It would be better if Violet and I went for a walk while you talk to the captain."

"Yes, I suppose so," Lily agreed.

"I'll be right back and let you know if a half hour from now is convenient with the captain," Ossie told her, and he hurried off down the deck.

Lily thought about what she would say to the captain. When it came right down to it, she didn't really know much about Wilbur Whitaker. She doubted she could be of any help as far as information about him was concerned.

And she was hoping Wilbur wouldn't somehow find out that she had talked to the captain about him. That might be dangerous.

Chapter Five
Captain's Investigation

O ssie showed Lily where to find the captain at his station and then he left with Violet to walk around the deck.

Lily found Captain John Donaldson to be a friendly, handsome man, tall, probably in his fifties, with a dimple in his chin and a smile on his face. His shoulders were broad, but he was not overweight and certainly not out of shape.

He immediately made her feel welcome as he offered her a small stool to sit down on. "Sorry, we don't ordinarily have ladies coming to visit, and I'm afraid that stool is the best I can offer you," he said with a big smile. He himself sat on another stool.

"This is fine," Lily told him, adjusting her long, full skirts.

"Now, in order to save you time, I'll just get right to the point," Captain Donaldson said. "I understand you have made the acquaintance of Wilbur Whitaker while you've been on this ship."

"That's right," Lily said. "I actually met him in the middle of the night when we had the bad storm." She continued, relating the other times she had seen him or talked to him. She ended with, "But I had never met him anywhere before."

"I see," the captain said thoughtfully. "And your friend Mr. Ossie Creighton told me you saw him with our late passenger,

Mr. Milford Ibson, and with another fellow, younger and well-dressed."

"That's right," Lily said again. "I never met the younger man and I don't know what his name is, but I saw them talking together twice, once on deck and once in the dining room with Mr. Ibson."

"I can't imagine what Wilbur Whitaker was doing in second-class, telling you he had the room occupied by Mr. Ibson," the captain said.

"I'm sorry I'm not much help," Lily said. "I was hoping you could give me some information about Wilbur Whitaker, because I would like to know why he is so interested in me."

"Yes, I understand. And we'd like to know if there's any connection between him and the deceased man that would be reason enough for him to have caused the man's death," Captain Donaldson said. "Our doctor thinks Mr. Ibson was beaten to death and then tossed into the ocean."

Lily gasped and said, "I'm so sorry about that man. He tried to talk to me on the deck that day, and I didn't know him so I made an effort to ignore him. He did say this would be his first time in the United States, but he didn't quite make it, poor man."

"He's listed on our register as a retired businessman, but we don't know what line of work he was in," Captain Donaldson said.

"So you do know the occupations of the passengers then?" Lily asked.

"Why, yes, but we don't have details," the captain said. "For instance, I looked up your name and find you're listed as the underage daughter of Charles Masterson, blacksmith and farmer."

"Then would you please tell me what you have for Wilbur Whitaker?" she asked.

"I've checked his name, too, and find he's listed as a farmer," he said. "When your friend came to me the first time asking for information on Wilbur Whitaker, I couldn't tell him even that much because it's against the rules to disclose anything at all about a passenger. However, in this case we have an investigation going on and we need all the help we can get."

"A farmer?" Lily questioned. "He told me he and his family live in town in Fountain Inn. How could he be a farmer and live in town?"

"That's a good question," Captain Donaldson said.

"He also told me his family has a lot of money and he didn't have to work," Lily added.

"We will check all information we obtain and we'd like to get back in touch with you—if not before we dock, sometime after you return home," the captain said.

"Yes, of course," Lily said. "I can give you my address—oh, but you already have that on my passport, I forgot. Anyway I'd be glad to help in any way I possibly can."

The captain stood up, and Lily rose from the low stool and quickly straightened her skirts.

"We appreciate that, Miss Masterson," Captain Donaldson said. "And I would advise you to avoid this Wilbur Whitaker, at least until after we finish our work on this matter. Thank you for coming and, if you think of anything else you might like to add, please feel free to call on me."

"Thank you, Captain Donaldson, for listening," she said. She turned to leave and the captain held the door open for her.

Lily found Ossie and Violet not far away, walking on the deck. She joined them and related her conversation with the captain. They paused at the rail.

"I'm afraid I didn't have anything worthwhile to tell the captain, and I didn't learn anything from him about Wilbur Whitaker except that the captain said he was on the ship's register as a farmer," Lily told Ossie while Violet stooped to watch the water below.

"A farmer?" Ossie repeated. "Maybe the family has bought a farm near Fountain Inn, but I can't remember any land for sale, at least not to outsiders. You know how the local citizens are. They don't want people from other places moving into the community, because they're afraid property values will go out the roof, and taxes as well."

"I specifically asked Wilbur where they lived, and he said within the town," Lily added.

"I could sense that the captain is suspicious of him, but of course he couldn't discuss him with me," Ossie said.

"Or with me," Lily said. She watched Violet sitting by the rail and continued, "He said he'd like to get back in touch with me."

"And with me," Ossie said. "Do you realize we will be docking in Charleston day after tomorrow?"

"Day after tomorrow?" Lily said, excited. "No, I really hadn't thought about it with so much going on. Oh, I'll be so glad to get home."

"I will, too," Ossie said. "I suppose you and Violet will be getting a train out of Charleston as soon as possible."

"Oh, yes, aren't you, too?" Lily asked.

"No, I have to get some information for Mr. Dutton in Charleston, and it may take a day or two," Ossie said. "I'm awfully sorry I can't go on home with y'all."

"What a disappointment," Lily said. "As soon as we met on the ship I figured you'd be going along with us after we docked."

"I sure wish I could, but it's not possible," Ossie said. "I won't be far behind y'all though."

"Wilbur had said he had to stay over in Charleston, too," Lily said. "So we won't have to avoid him when we get the train."

"Whatever you do, if you happen to see him just go in the opposite direction. And ignore him if he tries to talk to you," Ossie cautioned her.

Lily glanced over his shoulder and quickly dropped her gaze. "Don't look behind you, but I see Wilbur headed this way," she said under her breath.

"Remember what I was just telling you," Ossie said.

Lily looked down and saw that Violet was listening to what they were saying. "Get up and give me your hand so we can walk," she told the child.

Violet scrambled to her feet, and Lily grasped her hand.

"Yes, let's walk awhile," Ossie said.

Lily led the way in the same direction Wilbur was headed, hoping he would catch up and pass them by without stopping. She didn't dare look back.

After a few minutes of strolling along the deck, Lily said, "You'd think he would have passed us by now."

"The squinty-eyed man went inside that door back there," Violet said loudly, turning to point at a door behind them.

The three stopped walking and Lily asked, "Are you sure, Violet?"

"I saw him. You see, he's not behind us anymore."

Lily and Ossie looked back. There was no sign of Wilbur.

"Well, at least we avoided him this time," Ossie said.

"Let's just sit and relax for a while," Lily suggested. "I'm just plumb tuckered out." She fanned her face with her lacy handkerchief. ·

"I know it must be nerve-racking for you," Ossie said as he looked for three vacant chairs on the deck.

Everyone seemed to be outside, and it took a while to locate a place to sit. When three people vacated their chairs in a shady corner Ossie immediately claimed them.

Sitting down, Lily sighed with relief. Day after tomorrow couldn't come fast enough. She was anxious to see her father and to know how he was feeling. And she was anxious to get away from Wilbur Whitaker.

Things remained peaceful through the noon meal that day and on into the afternoon. Ossie had paperwork he needed to do in his room and he had left Lily and Violet sitting on the deck. Lily had rummaged in one of the trunks and found a different book for her sister, so she wouldn't get bored.

Violet settled down into her chair with the book, but Lily leaned her head back and closed her eyes.

"You are not going to sleep, are you, Lily?" the child asked.

Lily looked at her and smiled. "Oh, no, I wouldn't do that out here on the deck where people could see me," she assured her.

"Then I won't get sleepy, either," Violet said, and went back to her book.

Suddenly a man spoke from the other side of her chair, "It is a sleepy, lazy kind of day, isn't it?"

Lily turned quickly and saw the young man who had been with Wilbur sitting down next to them. Up close she could see he was probably around Wilbur's age but not so good-looking. He was much shorter, with black hair and black eyes and a thin black mustache. Now he was smiling at her.

Lily didn't answer but turned her head back in Violet's direction. Now, why did that man have to pick a chair next to them? More than likely, Wilbur would come along and join him.

"I'm sorry if you think I'm intruding, but since you are a friend of Wilbur, I thought nothing of speaking to you," the man said. "My name is Thomas Hickman. And I know from Wilbur that you are Lily Masterson, and the little doll sitting in the other chair is your sister, Violet. And you are from Fountain Inn, South Carolina, practically neighbors of Wilbur's family."

Before Lily could protest, Violet had jumped down from her chair and had gone to stand in front of the man. She placed her hands on her hips and announced with a frown, "I am not a doll. I am real."

"Of course, I'm sorry—" the man began, but Lily cut him short.

"We do not wish to converse with you, Mr. Hickman," Lily said forcefully yet in a polite manner. "Violet, get back up in your chair. And, Mr. Hickman, you please keep your words to yourself."

Violet sat back down.

"Well, well, well!" the man exclaimed. "And here I thought we were practically friends already."

"Your practicalities are not very practical, Mr. Hickman," Lily told him.

"Please accept my apologies," Mr. Hickman said, leaning forward.

At that moment Ossie suddenly appeared by Lily's chair and looked from her to the stranger and back again. "Is this man bothering you, Lily?" he asked.

Mr. Hickman stayed where he was, staring at Ossie.

"He thinks because I've met Wilbur that he can come along and act like an old friend," Lily explained.

"I apologized," Thomas Hickman told Ossie.

Ossie looked at him and spotted an empty chair on the other side. He pulled it over and placed it between Lily and Mr. Hickman, then he sat down on it.

"Since you are a friend of Wilbur Whitaker and Milford Ibson, the man who went overboard, what do you know about Mr. Ibson's death?" Ossie asked in a friendly manner. "Was he drinking, maybe?"

Lily knew Ossie was baiting the man, trying to get information.

"How do I know?" Thomas Hickman replied, fidgeting in his chair. "I certainly wasn't there when it happened. You know as much as I do about that."

"But the three of you were friends," Ossie insisted. "Had y'all been drinking together? Or had y'all even talked together right before the accident happened?"

The younger man looked at him sullenly and asked, "Who are you, mister? An investigator or something?"

"Oh, no, nothing like that," Ossie said smoothly. "I live near Fountain Inn where Wilbur's family lives. And, of course, I'm just curious about it all, same as everyone else has been talking about it."

"As far as I know, Milford Ibson just fell overboard and drowned," Thomas said with a frown. "And I know he did enjoy his liquor."

"Was he moving to the United States?" Ossie asked.

"No, I believe he was coming to our country to finalize some export business," Thomas said. "He owned a winery in France."

"Was he from France?" Ossie asked.

"No, he himself lived in England. The winery had been inherited from some French relatives," Thomas explained. He stood up and spoke to Lily, "I'm sorry I bothered you, Miss Masterson." Turning to Ossie, he added, "I've got to be going now."

He quickly disappeared down the deck.

"Ossie, you did sound like some kind of investigator," Lily said with a smile.

"You could have done the same thing," Ossie told her.

"No, he upset me too much with his brash attitude," Lily said.

"That's the secret of getting information," Ossie explained. "Friendly words usually elicit the answers you are looking for. Even though you might be boiling mad, cover it up with a smile and a kind word. I know that's hard to do sometimes, but it usually works and it's the best tool you can find for digging up hidden information."

Lily thought about that for a moment and agreed. "Yes, you are right. That's what I had planned to do with Wilbur to get information from him, but things got too deep and dangerous to take a chance."

"I'd say we probably know more about Mr. Ibson at this time than even the captain does, and I imagine if Wilbur learns his friend has been discussing the matter, he won't like it a little bit," Ossie said.

"So Mr. Ibson was only going to visit the United States," Lily said thoughtfully. "He did tell me this would be his first trip to our country. I suppose that meant he would be coming back again."

"Yes, if that was true about exporting wine," Ossie agreed.

Lily suddenly realized Ossie had returned much sooner than he had planned.

"You must have finished your paperwork in a hurry to be back so fast," she said.

"I decided that a lot of it can wait until I get into a hotel in Charleston," he replied. "I was worried about leaving you and Violet alone here on the deck. And I was right to worry."

"Oh, Ossie, I keep telling you I can take care of myself," Lily protested. "If that Mr. Hickman had insisted on sitting there, Violet and I would have left to walk around. I could have got rid of him."

"I wish I had asked him where he lives," Ossie said. "He had the same northern accent that Wilbur has, so maybe he's just visiting with Wilbur."

"Or he could have moved to Fountain Inn like the Whitakers have done," Lily added.

"Anyway I'm hoping he stays over in Charleston with Wilbur," Ossie said. "I don't want him on the same train with you and Violet. He shouldn't be allowed a single chance to irritate you."

"I hope he won't get the same train we do, too, but I'm sure a little word to the conductor would stop him from annoying us," Lily said.

She didn't let Ossie know, but she was concerned about the long journey from Charleston to Fountain Inn on the train, and then the problem of getting to her home in the country. Maybe she could find someone she knew in the drayline business and get a ride with them. Quite a few of her neighbors and friends hauled farm products to the city on a regular basis. And it was the time of year for the country people to be selling firewood to the city residents who would be stocking up for the winter.

"Can we take my dog on the train, Lily?" Violet asked.

"Your dog? Oh, goodness, don't let me forget to take your dog," Lily replied. Since Violet had only recently got the dog Lily was not used to looking after him, and now she was afraid she would completely forget him when they left the ship. Looking at Ossie, she asked, "What do I do with him?"

"You just check him in with your luggage on the train and they will put him in a baggage car where he'll stay until you get off," Ossie explained.

"Am I supposed to go in there to feed him and give him water?" Lily asked.

"Oh, no, you pay for that, and they'll take care of him," he replied.

"Then when we get off the train, I'll have to figure out how to get him home," Lily said. She smiled at Ossie and said, "You know, we've never had a pet animal before, and certainly not one that would travel with us."

"Once you get him home and he gets a little older, he'll make a good watchdog for Violet. She said he's only two months old and that he's a spitz," he said.

"That's right," Lily said and then added, "But I wish she had picked a kitten instead of a puppy. A kitten would be so much less trouble."

"But it wouldn't be any protection," Ossie said.

"You keep thinking we're in danger, don't you, Ossie?" she asked.

"It's safer to be careful when you don't know what kind of people you're dealing with," Ossie replied with a smile.

"Ossie, will you please hurry on home after you finish your business in Charleston? I'd like to know if you have any more news concerning Mr. Ibson or these other men. Also, the captain may contact me, and I'd like you to be there when that happens," Lily said.

"I'll leave for home the minute I finish. I promise you that," Ossie said. "And you be sure to talk to your father about all that's been happening."

"My father? If he's not too ill, Ossie. I don't even know how he is right now," Lily said sadly.

"I hope he's fully recovered when you arrive home," Ossie said.

"So do I," Lily replied.

She thought of her father's busy life. If he wasn't working in his blacksmith shop shoeing horses, he would be doing farm work. The chores never ceased, even though he had hired workers. He was the kind of person who would pay his bills before he would spend a dime for anything else, so during the last few years he had worked almost night and day in order to survive.

"While I think of it, you might check on my foreman for me and let him know that I will be coming home a day or two after you," Ossie said. "And, of course, Mr. Dutton knows where I am, that I am on this boat, and that I will stop over in Charleston."

"I'll be glad to," Lily promised. "It's going to feel so good just being back home again in our own house, with Papa there, and among our own kind of people. I couldn't understand half of what those people in England said."

Ossie laughed and said, "I know what you mean."

Lily appreciated her friendship with Ossie. He was always so understanding and kind. If she had had a big brother, she would have wanted him to be just like Ossie.

"I've been sitting so long that my legs have got crooked," Violet said, suddenly laying down her book and stretching as she stood up.

"You sound like a little old lady, Violet," Lily said with a laugh. She reached out to her. "Come here. I don't think I've hugged you today." Violet immediately reached her arms around Lily's neck as Lily squeezed her tight.

Then Violet turned, looked at Ossie, and said, "You, too, Ossie."

She hurried to hug him and almost knocked off his spectacles.

"Whoa, there," Ossie said teasingly, holding her close. "You're about to blind old Ossie here."

Violet stepped back and giggled. "You're not old, Ossie," she said. "You're my brother."

"I just wish I were," Ossie said, laughing.

Lily stood up and said, "I suppose Violet is giving us the hint that we need to walk. When we get off this ship we will have walked miles and miles."

"And that will be the day after tomorrow," Ossie reminded her.

Violet clapped her hands and jumped up and down as she cried, "We're going home! We're going home!"

Lily laughed as the three began to walk and said, "Of course we're going home. That's why we've been on this ship all this time, remember."

"But when we get off, then I'll know for sure that we're going home," Violet explained.

"Yes, and I'll know for sure then, too," Lily agreed. "This ship has been so slow that I feel like saying, hurry up, hurry up." She laughed.

* * *

During supper with Ossie, Lily saw Wilbur and Thomas come into the dining room and sit down at a table in the far corner.

"Both of them are back there," Lily said to Ossie.

Ossie and Lily were both sitting at an angle so they could observe the two men without seeming to do so.

"I suppose Thomas has reported to Wilbur that I asked questions this afternoon," Ossie remarked.

"Yes," Lily agreed.

They ate in silence as they watched the two men. Wilbur and Thomas seemed to be in a deep conversation about something as they bent their heads together over their meal. They didn't seem to be aware that Lily and Ossie and Violet were even in the room.

Suddenly, Wilbur pounded his fist on the table angrily and yelled, "I tell you I am not going to do it!"

"But you have to," answered Thomas in the same tone.

More conversation went back and forth between them that Lily and Ossie couldn't hear. Then once again, Wilbur pounded the table, causing dishes to spill. He stood up and shook his fist in Thomas's face as Thomas also rose.

"No! And I mean no! So don't ask me again!" Wilbur yelled at him.

"You will! I'll see to it!" Thomas yelled back and then quickly left the room.

A waiter rushed to rescue the dishes at their table, but when he tried to clean things up, Wilbur snatched the towel from the man's hand and threw it to the floor before rushing out of the dining room.

"My goodness!" Lily gasped in astonishment.

"The man is a lunatic!" Ossie said.

"Yes, and remember that the captain said Wilbur is in first class, so what is he doing down here eating in the second-class dining room?" Lily asked.

Ossie thought about that for a moment. "He probably has some good reason," Ossie said. "Like avoiding someone in first class, or hoping to get a chance to talk to you."

"I'll never talk to him again," Lily declared.

"I'm almost afraid to leave you and Violet in your room at night, for fear the man will find some way to get in," Ossie said, worriedly pushing his spectacles up on his nose.

"The lock works on the inside," Lily reminded him. "And not only that, I can push the trunks against the door for the night."

"Thank goodness, you only have tonight and tomorrow left on this ship," Ossie said.

Lily thought about that. She knew a lot could happen in that length of time. She didn't feel safe at all, but she wouldn't tell Ossie that. She knew him well enough to know he would probably set up camp outside her room at night if she mentioned her fears.

"In the meantime I don't plan to let you two out of my sight except for you to go sleep," Ossie declared.

"Ossie, I appreciate your concern, but I'm not even sure Wilbur Whitaker would want to talk to me, much less try to do us any harm," Lily said. "Remember he had asked me if we could become better acquainted during the rest of our voyage on this ship, but he hasn't even bothered to come speak to me. So evidently he has lost interest."

"I sure hope he has," Ossie replied.

And Lily hoped he had, too. She was definitely afraid of the man now that she had seen his temper flare.

Chapter Six
Home Again

After supper, Ossie walked with Lily and Violet on the deck until they were all tired. Then they sat down and watched the other passengers until the sun set and the sky became dark.

"I suppose I'd better get Violet to bed," Lily told Ossie when her sister began to nod in her chair.

"I will walk with you to your room to be sure you get locked in for the night," Ossie said, standing up from his chair.

Lily touched Violet's shoulder to wake her and said, "Come on, Violet. Time to go to bed."

Violet mumbled and rubbed her eyes, stood up, and held Lily's hand.

"I could carry you if you're all that tired," Ossie offered.

"I don't need anyone to carry me," Violet said, straightening up instantly. Then she looked up at Ossie and smiled, "But thank you anyway, Ossie."

When they arrived at their cabin, Ossie waited until Lily was sure no one was inside and then he told her, "I'm going to stand right here until I hear you lock the door inside. Don't come outside until I get back at seven in the morning."

"Thanks, Ossie. Good night," Lily replied, closing the door and fastening it.

"See y'all in the morning," Ossie whispered through the door.

Lily heard him walk on down the corridor. Then she quickly helped Violet undress and get into bed. She thought about pushing one of the trunks in front of the door and decided against it. On the one hand, Violet might start asking questions and getting scared, and on the other, Lily wasn't even sure she would be able to move the trunk.

After putting on her nightclothes, she got out her journal and found a pencil, then sat down on her bunk to record the day's events. As she wrote, she thought about happenings on the ship. Something seemed to be going on all the time, and she was tired of it all. She was so completely worn out, sleep overtook her.

Lily woke with a start when her head rolled to one side and she almost fell out of bed. Her notebook and pencil fell onto the floor and she sat up on the edge of the bunk. Reaching for her watch on the shelf by the bed, she gasped in surprise.

"One o'clock! My goodness! How could I just fall asleep like that?" she mumbled to herself. She looked up at Violet who was sound asleep.

She quickly picked up her notebook and pencil, then laid them on a chair. After a quick stretch, she pulled down the covers and jumped into her bunk. She left the lamp burning.

As soon as she got comfortable, she heard a clicking sound. She quickly glanced toward the door and saw the door handle slowly turning. Holding her breath, she sat up in bed and watched. There was no way someone could open the door from the hallway, because the bolt on the inside would hold firm, but just the same, her heart pounded so hard she could hear it in her ears. Who could be on the other side of that door?

Evidently whoever it was realized the door was securely bolted on the inside, so the handle turned back and she heard footsteps trail away down the corridor. She kept her eyes glued to the door until she could no longer hold them open, and she drifted off to sleep. The next thing she knew Ossie was knocking on the door.

"Lily, are you up yet?" Ossie asked from the hallway.

Lily stumbled sleepily to the floor and quickly replied, "Yes, Ossie, I'm up. Please give us five minutes to dress."

"Take your time. I'll wait right here," Ossie said.

Violet had also heard him and she slid down out of her bunk. "Must be . . . seven o'clock," she said between yawns.

"Yes," Lily assured her. She reached for a dress on a hanger and said, "Now, let's put this dress on. We'll get you ready so you can go outside and talk to Ossie while I finish."

Violet readily agreed to that. "And then we're going to eat breakfast, aren't we?" she asked while Lily buttoned the dress for her.

"That's right," Lily said, brushing her little sister's long blonde hair and tying it back with a ribbon. "Now you look fine." Calling to Ossie outside the door, she said, "Violet is coming out. I'll be along in two minutes."

"Fine," Ossie replied.

Lily opened the door just enough to allow Violet to slip through, then she closed it and began dressing herself. She realized she must have lost a lot of sleep the night before because she was so groggy this morning. When she remembered that someone had tried the door handle, she hurried to join Ossie so she could tell him about it.

She waited until they were all seated in the dining room and Violet's plate was piled with food before she turned to talk to Ossie about last night's event.

Sitting slightly sideways, to keep Violet from hearing her, she practically whispered, "Somebody tried to open our door last night."

"What?" Ossie exclaimed, almost choking on his coffee. He quickly set down his cup.

"It was right after one o'clock," Lily said, and she explained what had happened.

"We need to report this to the captain," Ossie said with a worried look. "I'll speak to him as soon as we're finished with our breakfast."

"I can't imagine who would have the nerve to try our door in the middle of the night. I don't believe Wilbur would do it, no matter what else he has been doing. Besides, why would anyone do such a thing?" Lily said. She laid her fork down.

Ossie reached out to cover her hand with his. "Lily, whoever was trying to get into your room was certainly up to no good. This really has me worried. I probably should sit outside your door tonight to be sure nothing happens to you and Violet."

"No, Ossie, I don't want you to do that," Lily said. "It was certainly frightening, but the inside latch is safe. There's no way anybody could open the door from the outside. Besides, we only have this one night left before we dock."

"Anyway, I am going to talk to the captain and ask him to see that one of the crew patrols the corridor by your room tonight," Ossie told her.

Lily slept better that night knowing that someone in authority was watching her door. She had stayed up late packing their belongings so the trunks could be moved out early the next morning. The ship was due to dock shortly after breakfast, and she would carry one valise containing the articles necessary for the train ride. Violet had her own little bag and her own tiny traveling suit, which Lily had made to match hers while they had lived in England.

When Ossie knocked on their door that morning, Lily was ready and waiting.

"We're all packed and ready for breakfast," Lily told him as she opened the door, smiling. "And nothing happened during the night."

Ossie blew out a sigh of relief and said, "Thank goodness! I have my things ready to be picked up, too. Let's go eat and get out on the deck in time to get a place where Violet can see when we sight land."

"I'll sure be glad to see the United States again," Violet said with a deep breath.

The dining room was becoming crowded by the time they got there. Other passengers seemed to be in a hurry, too. The waiter hurriedly seated them at a table near the door and placed their food on the table.

As soon as they had begun to eat, Lily looked up and saw Thomas Hickman coming through the doorway. She spoke to Ossie in a low voice, "Here comes Wilbur's friend, Thomas Hickman, and he looks madder than an old wet hen."

Ossie glanced toward the doorway and said, "Well, I hope this is the last time we see the likes of him."

Lily watched as Thomas was seated at a table for one across the room. "And he is eating alone," she said.

"He must be registered in our section," Ossie remarked. "And since Wilbur is in first class, I suppose he is getting ready to leave."

Thomas glanced in their direction several times with a surly expression, and each time Lily caught him looking at her, she felt her face burn. She was glad when they had finished their meal and left the dining room.

Ossie found a place for them near the rail where they could sit until the other passengers crowded the deck. Then they would have to give up their chairs and stand up.

"I am going to my cabin to get my bag first and bring it out here," Ossie told Lily. "Then I'll get yours and Violet's, so y'all just stay here where I know you'll be safe, and I'll be right back."

"Thanks, Ossie," Lily said as she and Violet sat down. As Ossie hurried back toward the door, she told her little sister, "Now you watch straight ahead and sometime soon we'll see the coast of South Carolina."

"Oh, it's so exciting to be going back home!" Violet exclaimed as she sat on her legs and stared out across the water.

Ossie was back in a few minutes and left his bag beside their chairs before he rushed off to get their valises.

Lily was excited about going home, too. She had missed her father, and she would even be glad to see his fussy old sisters. Aunt Ida May was all right, but Lily was always getting frustrated with her because she wouldn't stand up to her married sister, Aunt Janie Belle, who was much older and with whom she lived. Aunt Janie Belle ruled her home and her husband, who was getting senile now, with an iron hand. Aunt Ida May, an old maid, was younger than Lily's father. She would do anything to keep the peace. Lily never remembered a time when Aunt Ida May was not really afraid of her older sister's temper.

And Papa—oh, how glad she would be to see him. She just hoped he was well and strong by now, whatever had been wrong with him. And no matter what he said, she would never agree to leave him and go traipsing off to England again.

Ossie hurried up with their valises and broke into her thoughts as he set the bags next to his.

"That didn't take long," he said, taking a seat in a chair they had saved for him.

"Ossie, I really appreciate all you have done for us on this journey home," Lily said. "We might have been in some bad situations if you hadn't been on this ship."

"We're not saying good-bye yet, Lily," Ossie reminded her. "I'm going to stay right with y'all to see that you get on the train all right. And then, as soon as I finish my business for Mr. Dutton here, I'll be coming home."

"And I hope that won't take long," Lily replied.

The three sat silently watching more and more people crowd onto the deck until Ossie said, "I think we need to abandon these chairs now and stand at the rail. We'll probably sight land within the next thirty minutes or hour." He looked at the watch on the chain in his vest pocket.

Violet was becoming more excited, and Lily had to hold her hand to keep her sister from bouncing all over the deck after they had found a place at the rail. A few minutes later the ship's horn sounded. Violet jumped up and down while Ossie explained, "That means we've sighted land. You watch real close now and you'll see it."

Violet calmed down and pushed her face against the opening in the railing, until she finally saw the coast come into view. She was overcome with joy.

"That's the United States! Lily, that's where we live, in the United States!" Violet's blue eyes filled with tears of joy.

"That's right, dear," Lily told her. She looked at Ossie and said, "I didn't realize how happy she was about coming home."

Ossie smiled and said to the child, "Remember, that is the United States, but you still have to get on a train to go home."

"I know, I know," Violet exclaimed. "And I am never going to leave my home again."

"We won't have to, dear," Lily told her. "We'll stay home with Papa." She silently worried again about what condition she might find her father in.

"We'd better get in line now so we can leave the ship," Lily said, taking Violet's hand. The child picked up her small bag with her other hand. Lily reached down for her own valise, but Ossie quickly picked it up with his.

"It'll be all you can do just to hold on to her. I'll take your bag," Ossie said.

The crowd moved along, and soon the three were going down the gangplank. Lily glanced down at the crowd waiting to greet the passengers on the ship. No one would meet them because no one knew for sure when they would arrive. And not only that, since she didn't know who had sent the message and the fare, she was not sure who would even know they were coming home.

Ossie managed to get a hack after their luggage had been unloaded from the ship. "We'll go straight to the depot and find out when you will be able to get a train," he told Lily after the driver had loaded their luggage.

But Violet, looking back at the enormous pile of trunks and bags on the dock, suddenly remembered her dog. "I have to wait for my puppy!" she cried.

Lily and Ossie both stopped and looked at each other.

"She's right! I was about to forget the puppy," Lily said.

"I'm sorry," Ossie said, looking around. "I see crates over that way, and the puppy should be in that bunch."

Violet pulled ahead toward the direction he had pointed. As soon as she spotted animals in some of the slat-covered boxes, she rushed forward. She seemed to know exactly where to look. She stooped down in front of one of the large containers and began jabbering to the white puppy inside.

"We're going home, to our real home," Violet told the puppy.

She reached through the slats to pet the animal and said, "You be good now. We have to ride on the train."

The puppy was howling in excitement as he turned around and around inside the crate.

"I said you have to be good," Violet spoke firmly. The puppy stopped, looked at her, and wiggled his ears. "Now that's better."

Ossie stooped down beside the child to see the puppy. Looking up at Lily he said, "He looks like a thoroughbred spitz."

"He is," Lily said. "The farm where we got him had all kinds of puppies that they raise to sell."

"I'd say he's going to grow up to be a beautiful dog," Ossie said. He stuck his fingers through the slats, and the puppy came to lick them.

The man driving the hack followed them and asked, "Do you want me to take the puppy, too?"

"Yes, please," Lily said.

"Then you'll have to clear the animal through an office over there first," the driver said, pointing toward a wooden building nearby. "Do you have the papers for him?"

"The papers for him?" Lily questioned.

"The papers from the original owners telling where he came from," Ossie explained.

"Oh, yes, of course," Lily said. She rummaged in her valise and finally pulled out an envelope, saying, "Lucky I had them in here."

Ossie took the papers and told Lily, "You and Violet go ahead and get in the hack. I'll do this." He hurried toward the building.

The driver took Lily's valise and she and Violet followed him to the rig. By the time they were settled inside, Ossie joined them and said, "I cleared everything and made arrangements for the puppy to be shipped all the way to Fountain Inn, so you'll be rid of that much trouble. Now we'll go on to the train depot. And I hope you won't have to wait long for a train."

When they arrived at the depot and checked the schedule,

they found Lily and Violet would only have to wait about an hour for the next train.

"Why don't we get your luggage checked and then stop at the hotel with me long enough to drop mine and then get something to eat in that restaurant over there," Ossie suggested, pointing across the street where a "Cafe" sign hung.

"Fine," Lily agreed.

When they were finally settled in the restaurant across from the depot Lily relaxed a little and sat down to enjoy the home-cooked food. And, of course, Violet ate like she had not had anything to eat for the whole day.

The train came in early, and Ossie rushed to pay the bill. The three hurried across the street to the waiting train, where it sat huffing and puffing on the tracks.

The conductor allowed Ossie to take their bags inside and find seats for Lily and Violet. As they sat down and Ossie put their valises overhead, Lily said, "Thank you, Ossie, for everything. Please hurry home."

Ossie bent to squeeze her hand and look into her blue eyes with his dark brown ones. "I'll make it as fast as I can," he said. "Since we haven't seen hide nor hair of Wilbur and his friend Thomas, I'm hoping they won't show up on your journey home. But remember, if they do, just ignore them. And if that doesn't work, talk to the conductor." He bent and kissed her cheek, saying, "I'll see you soon." He planted a kiss on Violet's snub nose and left.

Lily removed her hat and took off Violet's bonnet. "Let's just get comfortable. We've still got a long journey ahead of us," she told her little sister.

This was only the second time Violet had been on a train, and Lily knew she would be excited most of the way, at least until she grew too sleepy to talk and look out the window.

But that wasn't long. By the time the conductor came through to collect the tickets, Violet was curled up fast asleep in her seat.

Late in the day, a man came through the aisle with a cart, selling food. Lily woke Violet so she could eat. The child ate again, but she immediately went back to sleep after devouring everything Lily had purchased for her.

Lily reached over Violet and pulled down the window as night came. The air was chilly, and she pulled a small blanket from her valise overhead to spread across both of them. Lily finally fell asleep to the rhythm of the train.

The next thing Lily knew, the conductor was coming through the car yelling at the top of his lungs, "Fountain Inn! Fountain Inn! All off for Fountain Inn! Next stop!"

Lily quickly woke Violet and gathered their things. As the train jerked to a halt, she held Violet's hand and hurried to the door. The child seemed to be walking in her sleep, but when she stepped down from the train and Lily pointed to the familiar sights of the town, Violet became wide awake.

"We're home! We're home!" Violet exclaimed, looking about the depot. "Where is Papa?"

"We're not quite home, Violet," Lily said. She led the girl down the platform to the depot. "And of course Papa wouldn't be here, because he doesn't know we're coming. Now, we've got to find a ride out to our farm."

Lily searched the crowd in the early morning light, but she couldn't see anyone she knew. Surely some friend would be here after hauling firewood in for the town's residents or on some other errand to the city. Finally she decided to speak to the stationmaster. Perhaps he knew who might be in town from the countryside where she lived.

Going into the waiting room, she found Mr. Gaines behind the glass window at the counter. She only knew him slightly, but she approached him and explained, "Mr. Gaines, I'm Lily Masterson, and I've just come in on the train. I wonder if you know of anyone who might be in town from anywhere near where I live out near Fairview."

"Oh, indeed, Miss Masterson," the man said, leaning forward to speak to her through the opening in the glass window. "I'm so glad you've come home. I heard that you and your little sister had gone to England to live with your aunt, but that's no place for a girl like you whose family has always been part of this community."

"Thank you, Mr. Gaines, I'm real glad to be back," Lily said with a smile. "But right now, you see, I need a way to get home. As far as I know, my father isn't aware that we've come back. Have you seen anybody who might be going out my father's way who would give my little sister and me a ride home?"

Mr. Gaines suddenly seemed completely confused, grappling to find words to speak. Whatever came over the man, Lily wondered. Maybe he was ill.

"Are you all right, Mr. Gaines?" Lily asked, anxiously bending to speak through the opening in the window.

Mr. Gaines straightened up, pulled at his tie, and said, "I'm all right, Miss Masterson. I suppose I'm just surprised to see you home." He turned to look at some papers on his desk behind him. "Now, let's see," he continued, leafing through the stack. "I don't see a soul from out your way." He turned to look at her and added, "But do you know Mr. Evans? I believe he lives way beyond where you do. He just brought in a shipment of wood to go to Greenville. And that wasn't too long ago, so he might still be around."

"I don't believe I know Mr. Evans, but if you can recommend him, I'd be glad for a ride with him if he is going near my house," Lily replied as Violet stood on tiptoes to look at the stationmaster above the counter.

"You just take a seat out there and I'll have somebody see if they can find him," Mr. Gaines said. He opened the door behind him and said, "I'll be right back."

As Mr. Gaines left his booth by the back door, Lily looked around the waiting room and sat down on one of the long benches that always reminded her of church pews. She pulled their valises up near her skirts and watched Violet, who was roaming the room to look at posters, and other passengers who were waiting.

Lily hoped Mr. Gaines would find Mr. Evans. She was this near home and wished with all her heart someone would give them a ride the rest of the way—and the sooner the better. She had a sudden feeling of urgency. Impatience was taking hold of her.

After a while, Lily saw a tall, older man in work clothes come through the front door to the waiting room. As he came closer, she noticed he had a wiry mustache, partly grey, that matched the grey hair poking out from under his wide-brimmed hat. His face was lined with wrinkles, and the wrinkles doubled when he smiled as he approached her.

"I'm Jake Evans," he said. "I believe you're Miss Lily Masterson."

Lily stood up and said with a big smile, "Yes, I am, Mr. Evans. I don't believe I've ever met you, but you may know my father, Charlie Masterson. You see, my sister and I have come home unexpected, and we need a way to get to the house."

"Yes, Mr. Gaines just told me," Mr. Evans said with a serious look. "I'd be awful glad to take you two home, Miss Masterson, if you're ready."

"Oh, yes sir, we are," Lily said. She motioned to Violet, who was standing across the room looking at them. "Come on, Violet. We're going to ride with Mr. Evans here."

"I have to warn you," Mr. Evans said. "I'm in my old wagon, and it might be purty chilly riding in it without a top. But I'll be glad to take y'all."

"Oh, Mr. Evans, anything you have to ride in will be fine. We're certainly glad to be able to get home whatever way we can," Lily said, reaching down to pick up the two valises at her feet.

Mr. Evans quickly bent down to retrieve the bags. "Here, let me do that, ma'am," he said. "Now if y'all will jest come this a'way, my wagon is behind the depot."

Lily started to follow him, but then she realized she had forgotten about their trunks that would be coming later. "Wait just a minute, please. I have to see about our trunks," she said as she turned back to the window. Mr. Gaines had returned and she spoke to him, "We have two trunks—"

"And a puppy," Violet interrupted.

"Oh, yes, and a puppy in a crate," Lily added.

She placed the baggage claim tickets on the shelf of his window, and he said, "Go ahead while you can get a ride. I'll see that you get your trunks." He looked at Violet, smiled, and added, ". . . and the puppy."

"Oh, thank you," Lily said. She turned back to follow Mr. Evans, who was waiting by the door to the platform.

Once in the wagon with Mr. Evans, Lily tried to talk with the man, but he didn't seem to be very talkative, so she finally gave up.

They traveled up the Laurens Road, and Lily explained where he should turn off. "It's not real far from this highway where the road begins that goes to our house," she said.

"Wherever it is, I'm glad to take you and your sister," Mr. Evans assured her as he left the highway.

Finally the private road that led to their house came into view, and Lily asked Mr. Evans to stop and let them off there.

"We've been sitting so long, I'd just like to walk the rest of the way," she explained to him, but he insisted that he should take them to the door.

Lily assured him it would be all right to leave them there. "You can't see the house from here, but it's just around the bend in the road there."

Mr. Evans stopped his horses, helped Lily down, and set her valises beside her.

"Are you sure you can manage these bags the rest of the way?" he asked.

"Oh, yes, I'm positive," Lily said with a big smile. She extended her hand to him and said, "I want to thank you with all my heart for bringing us from the depot. I'll tell my father, and I'm sure he'll be thanking you, too."

Mr. Evans seemed at a loss as to what to say. He shook her hand, cleared his throat, and jumped back onto the wagon, saying, "It has been my pleasure, Miss Masterson and Violet. Good day."

Mr. Evans drove away as Lily and Violet picked up their bags and began the walk down the road. Lily was happy, and Violet skipped along by her side.

How wonderful it was to be home . . . home to Papa!

Chapter Seven
Unexplained Accident?

The big two-story house came into view around the bend. Violet broke into a run, and Lily tried to keep up with her, but the valises slowed her down. The rose-bushes in the front yard were covered with late red blooms. The boxwood was neat and trimmed. And the tall oak trees had not yet lost their leaves.

Violet was already banging on the front door by the time Lily caught up with her.

"Is the door locked?" Lily asked. She set the bags down on the porch and tried the knob. It wouldn't open.

"We can't get in," Violet protested, again banging on the door with her small fists.

"Let's go around to the back," Lily said. "Maybe it's un-locked."

Leaving the bags on the front porch, Lily followed Violet down the cobblestone path to the rear entrance. That door was locked, too.

Lily looked around the backyard. "I don't understand why the house is locked up," she said. "Let's go down to the barn."

Violet ran ahead again, and when Lily finally caught up with her, she discovered that no one was there either. The horse and cart she always used were gone, too.

"Papa must have taken the cart and gone into town or somewhere," Lily said. She stood for a moment looking around. Their barn was near the border between her father's and Ossie's land. She could hear someone over there who was evidently talking to a horse. "I'm going over to Ossie's to see if Papa is there," she told Violet.

Violet, of course, was ahead of her all the way. When Lily walked through the hedges, she could see Violet talking to Ossie's foreman. He was holding the reins of a horse harnessed to a cart.

"We left Ossie in Charleston," Violet was saying.

"Hello, Roy," Lily greeted the short, plump man. "Yes, we left Ossie in Charleston, but he said to tell you he would be home in a day or two, just as soon as he finishes some business down there for Mr. Dutton. Roy, we are looking for my papa. Do you know where he is?"

The horse snickered and stomped his feet. Roy held tighter to the reins as he said, without looking at Lily, "Why, no, I haven't seen him today." Then he looked at her and said, "Why don't you just take the cart here while it's still hitched up and go over to your aunts' house. Maybe they could help you."

"Are you sure you don't mind?" Lily said, walking forward to take the reins. "Mine is not in the barn, so I suppose Papa is using it. Get in, Violet. We won't be gone long, Roy." They both waved back to him as Lily drove off to her aunts' house.

The two aunts lived down the road a piece. It was really too far to walk if you were in a hurry, and Lily *was* in a hurry. But even so, as she passed the boundaries of their property on the road, she noticed that the fields had already been plowed and wheat and barley sown. So she imagined the workmen were out clearing brush and dead wood on the backside.

As she drove by the separate road her father had cut to his blacksmith shop, she could see the shop building in the distance, but there were no horses in sight. In a few minutes they arrived at Aunt Janie Belle's house. Her father, who was Lily's grandfather, had given Janie Belle land and built a house to her specifications as a wedding present. And Aunt Janie Belle surely did have some specifications. The rambling two-story monstrosity was known far and wide as "Janie Belle's Mansion."

"I hope someone is home," Lily said as she pulled the cart to a stop in the front driveway.

"They are," Violet said, pointing to a window upstairs on the front. "I saw the curtain move up there." She jumped out of the cart and ran to the door. She couldn't reach the knocker, so she began pounding on the door.

Lily draped the reins around the concrete hitching post and followed. She ran to stop her little sister from knocking so hard.

"Wait, Violet, give them time to get to the door. Aunt Janie Belle won't like you making all that noise," Lily told her as she caught Violet's hand.

"Well, why don't they hurry up and open the door?" Violet exclaimed.

After a few minutes, Lily was wondering the same thing. Maybe they hadn't heard the knock. She lifted the knocker and tapped it hard.

"I know they're home because I saw the curtain move upstairs," Violet insisted.

"Maybe they have to get dressed to come to the door," Lily suggested. Just as she was ready to go around to the back door, she heard someone inside walking toward the front door.

The door opened, and Aunt Ida May appeared. "Lily!" she gasped in surprise. "What . . . how . . . why . . . ," she paused and stooped down to take Violet into her arms.

She held the child tight until Lily asked, "Why, Aunt Ida May, aren't you going to ask us in?" She laughed.

Her aunt stood up, still holding Violet, and Lily was shocked to see tears in her eyes. "What is wrong?" Lily asked, holding her breath. She sensed something was terribly wrong, and it had something to do with Violet and her.

Aunt Ida May tried to answer, but instead she motioned them into the house. They followed her into the small parlor off the front hallway, and before they could sit down, Aunt Janie Belle came into the room. She was asking her sister, "Ida May, I do declare. Who was it at the front door?" When the elder aunt saw Lily and Violet, she gasped and sat down in the nearest chair. "Oh, dear!" she exclaimed.

Even Violet could tell things were not normal by now. "Why is everybody crying and acting so sad?" she asked as she backed away from the others.

Lily quickly reached down to hold her tight. "Aunt Ida May, Aunt Janie Belle, where is Papa? He wasn't at the house," Lily demanded.

Aunt Janie Belle moaned and said, "Ida May, you tell them! I just can't!"

Ida May sat down on a chair behind her and said, "Lily, your papa is gone—"

"Gone?" Lily quickly interrupted and jumped to her feet. "What do you mean?"

"It was an accident, they say," her aunt explained. "He was shoeing a horse and—"

"Papa? Dead? Is that what you're trying to tell me? No, no, no!" Lily burst into tears and fell sobbing onto the carpet. Violet screamed, and Lily pulled her down into her lap.

"I don't know how y'all got home, child, but—" Ida May began.

Janie Belle interrupted, "Ida May, I told you to write to her and explain what happened."

Aunt Ida May stood silently weeping, a gentle hand on both Lily and Violet.

It was a long time before Lily could control her crying enough to ask questions. And Violet cried so much she got hiccups.

"When?" Lily managed to ask as she tried to control her voice.

"September second," Aunt Ida May replied as she tried to dry her own eyes.

Lily's mind did a quick calculation. September second was the date on the message she had received with the fare to come home. The word was that her father was ill. It hadn't said he was dead.

Lily wiped her tear-streaked cheeks and asked in a trembling voice, "Aunt Ida May, Aunt Janie Belle, do y'all know anyone by the name of Weyman Braddock?"

"Weyman Braddock?" Aunt Janie Belle repeated. "Why, no. Not that I can recollect. Why?"

"Neither do I," Aunt Ida May told her.

"I received a message at Aunt Emma's house in England that we should come home at once, and the fare for the journey was sent with it," Lily said. "It was signed by Weyman Braddock. Nobody knows who he is. And it was dated September second."

"That's strange," Aunt Janie Belle said as she shifted her hefty weight in the rocking chair.

"Very strange," Ida May echoed. "As far as could be determined, he died instantly."

Lily was still sitting on the floor and holding Violet in her lap. The child was sobbing softly now. Lily smoothed her tear-drenched hair back from her face.

"Why didn't y'all let me know?" Lily demanded, angry now when she thought about the way she and Violet had had to find out about their father's death. "He was our father and he was all we had—" She broke into sobs again and bent her head down against Violet's.

Aunt Ida May stooped down beside the two girls. She put an arm around Lily's shoulders and said, "I'm sorry, dear. I truly am. It was all so horrible, losing our only brother in that way, we just weren't thinking straight."

"We were going to write y'all," Aunt Janie Belle added. "And we were going to tell y'all and suggest you might as well stay on with your Aunt Emma. Your father's hired man, Logan, has agreed to take care of the farm for the time being until something can be done with it—"

Lily gave Violet to Aunt Ida May and rose quickly to her feet. "Something done with it?" she shouted. "What are you talking about? Selling it? That farm has been in our family since Revolutionary War days, and you know that. And as long as I live, I'll do all in my power to keep it." Lily was furious at the idea.

"Lily, calm down!" Aunt Janie Belle demanded, a little of her temper showing through. "Just what do you think you can do with the farm? You are a young lady. You can't farm the land. And you have to think of your little sister. She has to be taken care of."

Lily spread her feet and replied, "Aunt Janie Belle, you don't have to worry about us. I'll think of some way to save the farm. And as far as Violet is concerned, she comes first with me. Don't forget, I've taken care of her ever since she was born."

Ida May reached up to straighten Lily's skirts. "Lily," she warned, "let's don't say things we'll regret later."

Lily was immediately sorry for her outburst. "I apologize," she said, still sobbing. "It's just all so terrible, I can't even think straight. My dear Papa—gone!" She dropped to the floor beside Aunt Ida May, who put an arm around her.

"It'll all work out, dear," Aunt Ida May told her. "Remember, the Bible says, 'Ask, and it shall be given you.' We just have to put our trust in the Lord, and He'll take care of everything if we ask."

Lily's head was roaring, and her eyes weren't seeing. She was withdrawn into a swirl of sadness and misery. Her dear papa! She would never see him again around the farm, planting crops, or shoeing horses for the surrounding countryside. She had just lost her mother that very summer, and now her papa! How could she ever live through it all? What would she do now?

Then she realized Violet was speaking to her. "Let's go home, Lily, please," the child begged, tears still in her blue eyes.

Lily came back to the present. Violet was the most important person in all the world to her, and if she wanted to go home, then they would. She wondered how she could bear to walk around the house knowing her papa was no longer there, but she would do it for her sister.

"Yes, my darling, we'll go home," Lily told her in a shaky voice. She stood up and pulled Violet to her feet.

Aunt Janie Belle also stood up. "We want y'all to at least spend tonight with us," she said, laying a hand on Lily's shoulder. Her dark eyes looked directly into Lily's blue ones. "After all, we are the only kin you have here now."

Lily suddenly threw her arms around the woman's neck and

she sobbed, "Oh, thank you, Aunt Janie Belle. I do love you, but Violet wants to go home, and I think we ought to go. We'll come back to talk later."

Violet was pulling at Lily's skirt and Aunt Ida May held the child's other hand. "Lily, I want to go home," she wailed.

Lily quickly stooped and put her arms around her sister. "We're going home," she said. "Right now."

"There's no food in your house. Logan cleaned it all out for us and took it to his place," Ida May told her.

"That's all right, I'm not hungry," Lily replied.

"But the child, Lily," Aunt Janie Belle said. "You must have food or you'll both be sick. It'll only take a minute to get something together to tide you over until you can get to the store." She walked toward the hallway and Lily followed. Ida May and Violet followed them into the huge kitchen at the back of the house.

The two aunts found a stack of clean, washed flour sacks and began loading them with various supplies. Lily walked the floor, wishing they would hurry up. Then she remembered she had not seen Aunt Janie Belle's husband, Uncle Aaron.

"Where is Uncle Aaron?" she asked Aunt Janie Belle.

The elderly woman stopped pouring sugar into a bag and said, "He's been feeling right poorly lately and he sleeps a lot. He got up for breakfast this morning and ate and went right back to bed. He's getting old, Lily."

"I'm sorry, Aunt Janie Belle," Lily said. She knew the man was up in his eighties, and Aunt Janie Belle was not far behind.

"Let's don't forget the key," Aunt Ida May reminded her sister. "I don't imagine Lily has a key with her."

"No, I don't," Lily said.

"It's hanging on the nail just inside the pantry door," Aunt Janie Belle said.

Lily walked through the doorway and took down the key to her house. She squeezed it in her hand. This was the key to all her and Violet's future. Somehow she had to hold on to it. Some way things *would* work out.

After the aunts had gathered a few bags laden with groceries on the long table Aunt Janie Belle asked, "Now how did you get here? Did you walk?"

"Oh, no, I borrowed Ossie's cart from his foreman. Ossie was on the ship with us coming home. He had to stay in Charleston to finish some business for Mr. Dutton," Lily told them. She thought of her dear friend and wished she could talk to him right now.

"It's not time for Aggie to come in yet so we'll just help you put these in the cart," Aunt Ida May told Lily as she gathered up an armful of bags. Lily knew Aggie was Aunt Janie Belle's housekeeper.

Lily walked in a daze as they carried the things outside, told the aunts good-bye, and she and Violet left in the cart.

"I'll see you in the morning," Aunt Ida May called, waving to them as they rode away.

Later Lily would not be able to recall everything that her aunts had said, she was so deep in sorrow.

She pulled the cart to a halt at the back door, jumped down, and walked over to unlock the door. Violet followed close behind her. The key turned the lock and she stood there with her hand on the knob, knowing with all her heart she wanted to go inside, but hesitating. Violet, seemingly recovered from tears, pushed at the door.

"Open the door, Lily," the child said.

"Yes, dear," Lily said, turning the knob as she pushed the door wide open. Violet ran inside into the kitchen.

The first thing that met Lily's eyes was the leather apron her father wore when he shoed horses. It was hanging on its usual hook by the pantry door. She ran to it, hugged it tight, and the tears came again.

"Oh, Papa! Papa!" she cried.

Then Violet began screaming, "I want my papa! I want my papa!"

Lily immediately straightened up and turned to the child, who was clinging to her long skirts. She sat down in a chair and pulled Violet into her lap.

"I know you miss him. So do I, darling," Lily told her as she smoothed Violet's ruffled blonde hair. "But we can't bring him back. We have to get used to the idea that it's just you and me now." She tried her best to control her own tears.

Violet looked up at her and said, "We still have Ossie, when he comes home. Do you think we'll lose him, too, like Mama and Papa?" Her voice trembled and tears swelled in her eyes.

"No, we still have Ossie, dear, for this we should be thankful," Lily replied. "And I think you and I will get along all right as long as we have Ossie to advise us. Now, let's get the groceries inside so I can take Ossie's cart home." She helped Violet slide down to her feet.

Lily stepped out onto the back porch and saw Roy coming up the back walkway toward the door.

"I was watching for y'all to come back so I could come and help," Roy said. He stopped and stood before Lily. "I'm sorry, Lily, with all my heart. I want to do everything I can to help you out."

"Oh, Roy," Lily replied, and tears again blurred her vision. She fought for control. "You knew what had happened when we came by and got the cart, didn't you?"

"Yes, I did, but it was so unexpected to see you girls that I didn't know what to say," he said, shuffling his feet. "I could tell you didn't know a thing, and it wasn't my place to break the news. That's why I sent you all to your aunts."

"And, Roy, Ossie doesn't know either," Lily told him. "He left before it happened, didn't he?"

"That's right," Roy said. He glanced down at Violet, who was listening. He grabbed her up and tossed her into the air. "And how's my little sweetheart?"

"I'm not very good, Roy," Violet said sadly as he stood her on her feet. "Why do people I love have to go away and leave me?" She looked earnestly up into his face.

Roy glanced quickly at Lily and then stooped to face Violet. "But I haven't gone anywhere, have I? And you still love me, don't you?" he asked.

"You just don't understand, Roy," Violet said with a trembling voice.

Roy pulled her close to him and squeezed her. "I understand that I love you and your sister, and I know Ossie loves y'all, too. You and Lily are like my own daughters. I first knew you when you were born. Did you know that?"

That interested Violet. She leaned back to look into his face. "I can't remember that far back," she said. She looked at her sister and said, "But Lily does. She's told me all about me when I was a baby."

Lily walked toward the cart. "Let's bring all the supplies inside," she said. She couldn't bear to carry on ordinary conversation when her heart was breaking.

Roy insisted on bringing the food to the kitchen while Lily told him where to put what. When he had finished, Lily said, "Thank you so much, Roy. I appreciate your helping us, and also for letting me use the cart to go to Aunt Janie Belle's."

"Now, I want you to keep the cart and horse until Logan brings back yours," Roy told her. "He has one of his own, you know, and he just took yours home so he could look after the horse. I'll let him know y'all are home."

"Thanks, Roy. I'll put the cart in the barn in a little while," Lily said, looking around the room distractedly.

"I'll do that for you if you are finished with it for the time being," Roy said. "And I'll let the horse in the pasture behind the barn until you're ready to use it again. Is there anything at all that I can do for y'all? Anything?"

Lily looked at the man's concerned face and said, "Not right now, Roy. Maybe later. I want to be alone. I . . . I have to . . . get used to the idea that Papa is gone." Her voice trembled and she turned away so Roy couldn't see the tears.

"I'll just check with you now and then to see if you need me in any way. Is that all right?" Roy asked as he started for the back door.

Lily followed him to the door, reached for his hand, and said, "That would be fine. Thanks." She watched him go down the pathway to get the cart.

When she closed the door and turned back to look around the kitchen, she noticed Violet was no longer there. Her heart beat faster as she realized the child must have gone into the rest of the house, and she dreaded walking through the rooms where Papa had walked and to know she wouldn't find him there.

Taking a deep breath to steady herself, Lily stepped through the open door to the central hallway. "Violet," she said softly.

There was no answer, so she began looking into each room along the long corridor. The doors were all open, but Violet was not there. *She's gone upstairs*, Lily suddenly realized.

Lily's knees began to wobble as she slowly climbed the long, curved staircase to the second floor. How was she ever going to get herself under control? She had to, for Violet's sake. She stopped halfway up, squeezed her eyes shut, and took several deep breaths, which helped a little.

Lily straightened her shoulders and got to the top, then she began looking for Violet in the rooms upstairs. But she was nowhere to be found. Then Lily knew she had one last place to look, Papa's office at the end on the back side of the house. She walked in that direction and found the door was closed.

Slowly turning the knob, Lily pushed the door open and found Violet sitting in Papa's big chair, with his pipe in her small hands. She was crying so hard she shook all over.

"Violet, darling!" Lily said, stepping inside and quickly reaching for the pipe.

"No!" Violet screamed at her as she held the pipe close to her.

Lily had had to comfort the child during the loss of their mother, but Violet had never really known her mother very well because of the illness that had completely disabled her for years. And the child seemed to quickly recover from the death. But now this was an entirely different matter. Violet had been her father's little shadow and had followed him everywhere he would allow.

While Lily stood there at a loss, she remembered Aunt Ida May's words, "Ask, and it shall be given you." She silently asked the Lord, "Please help me to know what to say or do."

She continued standing there, looking at Violet, and she noticed the child seemed to be completely worn out. "Violet, let's you and me go take a nap," she said, and quickly added, "We can go to my room and lie down on my big bed, like we do when there's a thunderstorm, all right?"

Violet considered this idea for a moment and finally said, with a sob, "Can I take Papa's pipe with me?"

As much as Lily would have liked to leave the pipe in the office, she readily agreed. "Yes, but you'll have to be real careful with it," Lily said.

Violet stood up and, holding the pipe in both hands, followed Lily to her bedroom.

Lily quickly looked around. The bed was made just like she always kept it, and her books were still in the bookcase by the bed. She was about to look into the wardrobe to see if there was something there she could put on, but then she remembered their bags were still on the front porch.

"Violet, do you want to stay right here while I go get our luggage from the front porch? We forgot it, didn't we?" she asked the child, who was now sitting on the side of the bed.

Violet jumped up and carefully placed her father's pipe on the bedside table. "No, I'll go with you," she said.

They retrieved the bags and brought them up to Lily's room.

"Let's see what we can find for you to put on while you take your nap," Lily said as she opened the valises and pulled out the garments they had brought with them while Violet watched. Lily held up a blue robe she had made for her little sister in England. "How about this? We'll just take off your dress and put this on, and then climb into bed for a short nap." She stood up.

"What are you going to put on?" Violet quickly asked. "If I am going to take a nap, you have to, too."

"Oh, I have a robe there in my bag that I'm going to put on," Lily replied. She bent over to help Violet remove her dress.

Once she had the blue robe on, Violet didn't object when Lily turned back the covers and told her to hop in. But she watched every move Lily made as she took off her dress and put on a loose-fitting housedress.

Violet frowned when Lily lay beside her and asked, "You won't go off and leave me if I go to sleep, will you?"

Lily reached to smooth the child's hair and said, "Of course not. I'm tired, too."

"If you do, I'll know about it," Violet said. Then she scooted down beneath the covers.

"I promise," Lily said as she reached for Violet's hand.

Violet was soon asleep. Lily turned on her side, facing away from her, and wondered what their fate would be without Papa. Tears silently fell upon her pillow. Her thoughts became jumbled and, after a long time, she finally fell asleep.

Chapter Eight
Helpful Visitors

A hammering noise was going through Lily's head. She suddenly woke and realized someone was pounding on the front door. Her room was on a front corner of the house, and she hurried to look out the window to see who was below. Logan was standing down there beside her horse and cart, and as she watched, Roy stepped back from the door to where she could see him.

"I'll be right down," Lily called to the men, and then quickly grabbed her dress and put it on.

She glanced at Violet and was surprised to see the child had slept through the commotion. She had promised not to leave while she was asleep, but she hated to wake her. Then she figured she'd better keep her promise.

Touching Violet on the shoulder, Lily said softly, "Violet, I have to go downstairs. Logan is in front of the house with our horse and cart, and Roy is with him."

Violet immediately sat up, rubbed her eyes, and jumped out of bed, removing the robe as she went. Lily helped her into her dress.

"I'm going downstairs, too," Violet declared as she dressed.

"All right, let's hurry," Lily told her as she tied the child's sash.

When Lily opened the front door, she saw Logan coming up the walkway. She was overcome with grief and couldn't speak. The elderly man put his arms around both her and Violet, and not a word was spoken.

After a few moments Lily wiped her eyes with her handkerchief and stepped back to look at Logan. He had worked for her grandfather, who had died when she was only five years old, but she could remember him. Grandfather Thaddeus, "Tad" he was called, used to take her fishing, and Logan always came along. Grandpa Tad had called her his "Tadpole," and now Logan reminded her of these pleasant memories.

"Tadpole, what can I do?" Logan asked. He looked at her with tear-filled eyes, and ran his wrinkled hand through his thick grey hair.

"Oh, Logan, I just don't know," Lily said. "If I can get my mind straightened out, I need to talk to you about the farm."

"Not now, not now," Logan said. "Everything's being taken care of. There's no need to get in a hurry. Jes' take it easy fur a while and let things settle down."

Logan continued holding Violet's hand when Lily straightened up and glanced out at the cart where Roy remained standing. She saw their trunks on the cart.

"Y'all brought our trunks," Lily said.

"And a mite of a puppy they said belongs here," Logan said, smiling down at Violet.

Violet frowned, looked up at him and then out toward the cart. Finally she said, "I suppose he can stay here awhile, as long as we do."

Lily was shocked to hear her talking that way. She would have to remember not to discuss things in front of her anymore. Stooping down, she said, "Violet, that will be an awfully long time. Now come on, let's go get him."

Violet still didn't look anxious to see the puppy she had been so excited about earlier, but she allowed Lily to take her hand and lead her out to the wagon.

Roy saw them coming and he hastily opened the crate on the cart and took out the white puppy. "Look what we brought," he said to Violet, holding it out to her. The puppy was squirming and squealing to get down.

The child looked up at the little animal a moment and then she said to Roy, "Just put him down, please." She stood back to wait.

Roy, Logan, and Lily all looked at each other over the child's head, and then Roy carefully placed the puppy on the ground near Violet's feet. The puppy ran around in circles for a moment, smelling everything, and then he went straight for Violet's feet and began gnawing at her shoes.

Violet sat down on the cobblestones and bent to look at the puppy, "Now, I told you that you have to be good," she said, shaking her finger at him.

The others drew a breath of relief and again looked at each other. Lily walked around to rub her horse's head as he stomped his foot and whinnied. He still knew her. "Lightnin', I'm home," she whispered.

"Now whereabouts you want these here trunks?" Logan asked.

"Could y'all possibly bring them upstairs?" Lily asked as she looked at the huge trunks.

"Sure can," Roy said. "And we'll put the crate in the kitchen for the puppy."

Lily led the men up the steps, and Violet followed carrying the puppy.

"If you'd just put them in the hallway here at the top of the steps I can unpack them later and put them in the attic," Lily told the two men, who deposited one trunk there and went back down for the other one and the large valise she had checked on the train.

When they were finished, Roy told her, "Now, you just let me know when you get these emptied out and we'll come back and move them to the attic."

"Thank you, Roy," she said. They all went back downstairs, and the men put the crate in the kitchen near the cookstove where the puppy could stay when it turned cold.

"I'm going to put your cart in the barn and let Lightnin' out in the pasture behind the barn. Roy will get Ossie's down there and take me home," Logan told her.

"I didn't even think to ask," Lily said. "How did y'all happen to bring the trunks?"

"I had to go into town to pick up tobacco," explained Roy, "and I ran into Logan here. He had been to the depot to get some seed that had come in."

"And Mr. Gaines at the depot had told me your luggage was waiting to be delivered, so we jes' put it on the cart," Logan finished.

"Well, I sure do thank both of you," Lily said.

"You're much obliged," Logan called back as they went back to the cart. "I will see y'all tomorrow."

Violet spoke to the puppy in her arms, "We're going to have company tomorrow. Now, you remember to be good, you hear."

Lily glanced at the grandfather clock sitting in the front hallway next to the stairway. Noontime already! Evidently Logan or someone had been keeping it wound.

"Come on, Violet, let's get something to eat," she told her little sister as she walked toward the kitchen.

Violet followed, and dropped the puppy onto the straw bed in the crate. He started whining.

"He's probably hungry," Lily said. She looked around the kitchen and noticed that firewood and kindling were neatly stacked behind the big iron cookstove just as though things were normal. She quickly made a fire in the stove and began preparing some food.

"What does a puppy eat?" Violet asked as she watched the tiny animal.

Lily stopped for a moment to think and then said, "He'll probably eat whatever cats do. Remember, we had a cat one time that ran away? So I'll save him the scraps from our dinner."

Rather than take the time to bake biscuits, Lily cooked flapjacks in the iron frying pan and warmed a slab of ham in the oven. The whole time she was silently thanking her aunts for insisting that she bring food from their house. She found a jar of green beans among the things they had given her and a large jar of homemade grape jelly. These would all make a good meal for them.

While she was busy cooking, Lily felt hungry, but once everything was done and on the table, she wasn't sure she'd be able to eat.

"Wash your face and hands now. Everything is ready," she told Violet, who was still playing with the puppy. "And be sure you put—what is his name, Violet? Puppies have to have a name." She turned to look as Violet deposited the puppy in the crate again.

"A name?" Violet said, standing up. She thought for a moment and then said, "I'll have to think about that." She went to climb up onto the stool at the sink to wash.

Violet had her own special stool with a back that her father had made for her just this year, so she could reach the table without sitting in the old highchair, which she had outgrown. She climbed up and sat down as Lily pulled out a chair on the other side of the table and sat there.

Lily looked across at her little sister, who had bowed her head and was evidently waiting for thanks to be returned. Papa had always said the blessing, but now she must do it.

"We thank Thee for this food, dear Lord, and for all our other blessings," Lily said. She almost choked on the "Amen."

Violet's appetite had returned and she began requesting some of everything. Lily was glad to see this, but she had to force herself to eat. Nothing seemed to have any taste, and food was hard to swallow.

As usual, Violet was silent while she was eating, and that left Lily time to think. She needed to do something, just anything to occupy herself, but what? She could make a list of all the food her aunts had given them and then make another list of what she needed from the store. But she didn't feel up to going to the store, which was about two miles down the road at the forks, because people would be there who would extend sympathy, and she didn't want that right now.

Maybe she could unpack the trunks—yes, that's what she'd

do. And Violet would probably want to help, so that would occupy her for the time being, too.

When she got the table cleared and everything put away, Violet wanted to give the puppy the scraps.

"Take him outside to eat. He's little, and he might mess up the floor," Lily told her little sister. "Just set his plate right down there by the porch and you can sit on the steps and watch him to see that he doesn't run off."

Violet carefully placed the plate by the walkway, brought the white puppy outside, and stuck his nose in the food. He began eating as though he were starved while Violet sat on the bottom step and watched.

Lily set a bowl of water by the steps and then waited inside the doorway. When he had finished every bite, she told Violet, "Let him run around for a few minutes and then you can bring him back in."

Violet played with the puppy and he became excited and barked loudly as he followed her about the yard. Finally they both grew tired, and Violet brought him back in and put him in the crate.

"He sure can make a loud noise for such a small puppy," Lily remarked, forcing a smile.

"He thinks he's talking to me, but I can't understand a thing he's saying," Violet said with a serious look on her face. She looked down at him in the crate and said, "I think he needs a nap."

Lily looked at her and asked, "Do you want to take a nap too?"

"No, I already had a nap," Violet insisted.

"That's fine. Then you can help me unpack our trunks," Lily said.

"Oh, yes, let's do that," Violet agreed.

Luckily all their clothes were clean when they left England, so now everything they had not worn on the trip could be hung up. As they filled the huge wardrobes in their adjoining rooms, Lily realized they had more clothes than she could ever remember. But that was because her Aunt Emma had purchased bolts of material for Lily to make everything from nightgowns to Sunday dresses, and she had done nothing but sew during most of their stay in England. She silently thanked Aunt Emma for all these wonderful clothes.

Then Lily realized she should sit down and write to Aunt Emma because she would be anxious to hear about Papa. She promised herself she would try to compose a few lines to her tonight after Violet went to sleep.

After a while, Lily looked into both trunks and said, "I believe we have got everything out. They're both empty."

"Can I go play with the puppy now?" Violet asked. "Outdoors?"

"Outdoors?" Lily repeated as she closed the lids on both the trunks.

"He likes to smell everything outside and scratch in the dirt," Violet explained.

"All right," Lily said. "Just let me get some paper and a pen to take with me, and we'll go downstairs." She looked into the cubbyhole over the long table in her room and, sure enough, her bottle of ink and a pen were still there. Taking them and a few sheets of paper from the drawer, she followed Violet down to the kitchen.

Violet picked up the puppy and Lily said, "Now I'll just leave the door open and I'll sit right here at the end of the table so I can see you." She opened the door, and Violet carried the puppy outside. Then she sat down at the table to write that note to Aunt Emma.

She tried and tried to collect her thoughts enough to begin the letter, but she couldn't bring herself to put down in black and white the sad facts. She watched Violet, but her mind was far away.

Suddenly the puppy began barking loudly, bringing Lily back to reality.

"What is wrong with him?" she called to Violet.

"Somebody is coming, and I think it's Aunt Ida May," Violet said, watching as the puppy kept barking in the direction of the road.

When the cart came closer, Lily could see that it was Aunt Ida May. Lily was really glad she had come. She wanted to talk about things now, and Aunt Ida May was one person she could discuss things with, provided Aunt Janie Belle was not present.

Lily watched from the doorway as the lady stopped the cart beneath a tall oak tree and threw the reins over the hitching post. Violet ran to greet her, with the puppy barking at her heels.

"My, my, what a dangerous puppy!" the lady exclaimed with a big smile as Violet ran to her.

Violet stooped and picked up the puppy. "He's not really dangerous, Aunt Ida May," she said. "He just likes to make noise."

Lily waited in the doorway for her aunt to come inside. She was carrying some packages, and from what Lily could see, the cart held lots more.

"I know I said I'd see y'all in the morning," Aunt Ida May said as she deposited her load on the kitchen table. "But Janie Belle and I got to talking and we decided you might need some more supplies, so here I am, come to stay a few days, if you'll have me."

Lily embraced her aunt and said, "Aunt Ida May, you didn't have to bring all this stuff, and of course you are welcome to stay as long as you like."

They walked back to the doorway and Lily saw Roy coming across the yard.

"Hello there, need some help?" he called to Aunt Ida May.

"At my age I can always use help," Aunt Ida May replied with a big smile, walking with Lily to pick up another load from the cart. "If you don't mind, I need all this taken into the house."

"I'll be glad to do it," Roy said, and he began by grabbing packages and a large valise from the cart.

"Oh, I forgot to warn you. There's eggs in there somewhere. Janie Belle put them in, and I don't know where they are," the lady explained.

"I do hope I haven't broken them," Roy said as he started toward the kitchen with his arms full. "I'll be careful."

When he had finished bringing everything in, there was

enough to cover the long kitchen table. Lily looked at it and then at her aunt and said, "Aunt Ida May, we can't possibly use all this stuff. You must have brought half of everything y'all have."

"Not hardly," Aunt Ida May said. She turned to Roy and said, "If you'd be good enough to get your men to return the cart and horse to Janie Belle for me, I sure would appreciate it. I've come to stay a few days."

"I'm glad you have, Miss Ida May," Roy said. "And I'll take care of the horse and cart. Let me know if there is anything else I can do."

He started to walk back toward the cart and Lily asked, "Roy, how did you happen to know Aunt Ida May was here?"

Roy looked at Violet, who was standing nearby holding the puppy, and he said, "It was that ferocious dog there barking like he was going to eat somebody up. He sure makes a good alarm." He pretended to be serious, but a smile twisted the corners of his lips.

"He didn't know Aunt Ida May, and he was trying to get acquainted with her," Violet said, looking down at the squirming puppy in her arms.

"Well, I hope he knows her now," Roy teased. And then he told Lily, "I believe he will eventually grow into a good watchdog."

Lily smiled and said, "That's exactly what Ossie said on the ship."

Aunt Ida May looked at her and asked, "You had that puppy on the ship?"

"We bought him from Aunt Emma's neighbor in England and brought him all the way across the ocean," Violet said. "And he rode the train, too. Roy brought him from the depot with Logan."

"For goodness sakes!" the aunt exclaimed. "All the way from England. Don't let your Aunt Janie Belle know where he came from or she'll be calling him a 'furreigner,' as she says it."

"I won't," Violet promised, and she ran out into the yard to put the puppy down.

Roy climbed up on the cart and yelled back, "Holler if you need me," before he turned and drove the vehicle down the driveway.

Lily and Aunt Ida May went back into the kitchen, where the lady quickly removed her hat and gloves and went to work on sorting the pile on the table. "We need to find those eggs," she told Lily.

Lily suddenly realized there were no chickens inside the fence by the barn. Papa had always kept lots of chickens. And then she wondered where her father's cattle had gone, if any were left on the property.

"Aunt Ida May, what happened to all of Papa's livestock?" she asked while they sorted through the stacks.

"Why, nothing, child," Aunt Ida May said. She paused over a bag and examined it to see what it contained. "Logan just moved everything down to the far end of your land so it would be nearer his house, where he could see to it better. Remember we told you Logan had agreed to take care of everything."

"I'm sorry. I guess I forgot what all you said," Lily said as she picked up a bag and found it full of sweet potatoes.

"Now we need to put all this stuff in some order in your pantry so you will be able to find things when you want them," Aunt Ida May said. She opened the door to the huge pantry and looked inside. The room was almost as large as the kitchen.

With both of them sorting and carrying, it didn't take long to transfer it to the pantry. And the last bag Ida May picked up contained the eggs.

"Well, here they are," she said as she took a large bowl out of the bag and set it on the table. It was full of eggs nestled in salt to keep them fresh. "We'd better put them in the pantry to keep them away from the heat of that stove there," she added. She took the bowl over and placed it on a shelf.

"Now, Aunt Ida May, I'll take you upstairs so you can hang up your things and freshen up," Lily told her. "But, first, let me tell Violet, so she'll know where we are."

Violet was having a good time playing with the puppy in the

yard and when Lily called to her to tell her that they were going upstairs, she said, "I'll stay out here awhile."

Lily showed her aunt to the company bedroom and helped her empty her valise. While she worked, she was thinking about what to ask Aunt Ida May concerning her father.

"I'm ready to go back downstairs where we can sit and talk awhile," the aunt said.

"So am I," Lily agreed, so they went downstairs to sit at the kitchen table, where they could see Violet outside.

"There are so many things we need to talk about, Lily," Aunt Ida May said.

"Yes, I know," Lily said. "And, Aunt Ida May, there are so many questions I want to ask. I feel like I can talk about things now."

"That's good, child," Aunt Ida May said. "I've always said talking about things helps us to understand."

Lily wanted to know everything now. She didn't want to sit and wonder. Somehow she'd begin asking questions. The answers might sorely hurt but she needed to ask the questions.

Chapter Nine
Ida May's Story

Lily stared at the wooden floor in the kitchen for a few moments, then she raised her head, took a deep breath, and said, "Aunt Ida May, please tell me . . . everything . . . what you know . . . about . . . that day."

"Child, I'm afraid I don't know a whole lot about that day," Aunt Ida May said, and then she added as she looked directly at Lily, "except that I was the one who—ah, found your father."

"Oh, tell me, Aunt Ida May, how it all was," Lily said softly as her father's face floated through her mind, kind, smiling.

"Janie Belle and I had been baking bread all morning and we thought perhaps your father could use some of it," Ida May began. "And you know Janie Belle's feet bother her and she was tired. So I said, well, I'll just take two loaves over to Charlie, while Aggie cleaned up our kitchen." She paused and looked at Lily.

Lily waited, anxiously listening for the next word.

"Well, I didn't even get cleaned up myself but jumped in the cart and hurried over here before the bread got cold," Ida May continued. Her dark eyes took on a faraway look. "When I passed the road to the blacksmith shop I could see there was a fire going in the forge and one of your horses was tied to the hitching post." She paused again. Looking down at her skirt, she began smoothing the folds. "I drove down to the shop, and the first thing I saw was . . . was . . ." She cleared her throat and continued, "was Charlie lying there on the ground." She cleared her throat again and looked at Lily.

Lily slid off her chair and came to kneel in front of Aunt Ida May as she grasped the woman's hand. She realized in all her misery that it hurt her aunt to have to recall the facts. Ida May reached to smooth Lily's blonde hair.

"Did you—was he—?" Lily couldn't bring herself to ask the question.

"I jumped down and ran to him, Lily, but even before I touched him I could tell . . . it was . . . too late," Ida May continued. "It hit me so hard and so unexpectedly that I must have screamed at the top of my lungs until finally Logan came down the road to the shop." She took several deep breaths.

"You said . . . they declared it an accident, Aunt Ida May," Lily said in a trembling voice. Tears ran down her cheeks. "Did it look like an accident?"

Ida May straightened up in her chair and said, "The sheriff said it was an accident, and that apparently he had been kicked by a horse, but there was no horse there except one that belonged to him and it was tied up a good distance from where he lay."

"How did they decide a horse had kicked him? Where had the horse kicked him?" Lily asked, squeezing her aunt's hand in hers.

"They claimed, dear—and this is something I hate to tell you —but they claimed the horse had trampled him because of the shape he was in. He was almost unrecognizable from all the damage done," Ida May explained.

Lily quickly got to her feet and began walking around the kitchen. Then she stopped and looked directly at her aunt and asked, "Aunt Ida May, please tell me. Do you yourself think a horse killed him?"

Ida May was quick to answer that. "No, no, I don't," she said. "But there is no way to ever find out if that was what happened, Lily."

Lily whirled around and walked to the other end of the kitchen and turned back to look at her aunt. "I don't believe my father was . . . killed . . . by a horse, Aunt Ida May. He was too much of an expert in his work. You know that," she said. "Not only that, if the story was true, where was the horse who did it? Did they find out whose horse he was shoeing when it happened?"

"No, child, they never did, but then, who would admit their horse did such a thing?" the aunt said. Her voice was edged with anger as she added, "And that sheriff just decided there was nothing to investigate. He just decided on this story and didn't even try to follow through on anything. I talked to him myself several times and every time I got the same answer. A horse had been responsible and that was it."

"You said Logan came to the shop while you were there," Lily said as she sat back down. "What did he think?"

"He thought there ought to be an investigation, that your father was too good a blacksmith for it to be an accident," Ida May replied. "In fact, quite a few people here in the country who knew your father were surprised that the matter was not investigated thoroughly."

Lily leaned toward her aunt and said softly, "I have a feeling, right here"—she patted her heart—"that something is wrong, that my father died from something besides a horse."

"So do I, child, but what can we do?" Ida May said, sadly shaking her head.

"I don't know right now, but I will not rest until I have heard all the details from everybody involved," Lily said. Then she remembered the date of the message she had received in England. "Aunt Ida May, whoever this Weyman Braddock is, who sent me the message and fare to come home, he must be found. The message asked me to come home at once, that my father was ill, and all the time he was already d . . . dead. It was dated September second."

"Braddock is an unfamiliar name in this part of the country," Ida May told her. "I can't imagine who he could be and, not only that, why would he send you a message?"

Lily suddenly had an idea and she anxiously asked her aunt, "Do you think this name, Weyman Braddock, could be a name someone made up to keep his identity from being known?"

"I just don't know, child," Ida May said. "Why would someone not want to put their real name on a message?"

Lily thought for a moment and then she said, "I think the real question is, why would *anyone* send me a message that my father was ill when in fact he was . . . already . . . gone?"

Ida May reached over to pat Lily's hand where it rested on the table. She said, "I know this is hard to accept, but it's all done and over with, child, and there's no use in making yourself sick over what actually happened. It won't bring your father back."

Lily pursed her lips and frowned. "No, it won't bring Papa back," she said in a quivering voice. "But I don't think I can live the rest of my life without trying to find out exactly what happened, Aunt Ida May."

"If there was a person involved in this, Lily, you must remember that it could be dangerous for you to go around asking questions and stirring things up," her aunt told her.

"I'm not worried about the danger. I can take care of myself," Lily said. "But Papa is not here to take care of whoever was involved, and I'm sure someone was responsible, not just a horse."

"Well, if you're so determined, please promise me, dear, that you will keep me informed," the aunt said. "And please don't do anything foolish."

"Aunt Ida May, you and Ossie are the only people I ever confide in about anything, and Ossie is not home yet," Lily said. "But I do want to talk to Ossie just as soon as he returns. I hope you can stay here with us for a long, long time. It would mean so much to have you to talk to."

Ida May smiled at her and said, "I'll be here as long as you need me, child." She stood up and looked at the iron cookstove. "Why don't I just make us a pot of nice strong coffee? I think it would clear our heads a little." She walked over and took the pot from the shelf while Lily got the coffee out of the pantry.

While the pot percolated, Lily sniffed the air and said, "It sure smells delicious." Looking toward the doorway, she remembered her sister and said, "I need to check on Violet."

Violet was still occupied with the puppy. She was now playing a game of hide-and-seek with the excited little animal. Lily was grateful the child had something to keep her young mind off the tragic event they had come home to. She stood and watched her little sister.

"I do believe it's strong enough now, Lily," Aunt Ida May called to her from where she stood by the stove.

Lily quickly turned back inside and said, "I'll get some cups." She went to the large china cupboard at the end of the room and brought two cups and saucers to the stove.

Aunt Ida May carefully poured the hot liquid and they took their coffee to the table, where they sat down.

"Ummm! Tastes good!" Lily said, smiling at her aunt as she sipped.

"It is pretty good even if I did make it," Ida May agreed with a little laugh.

Lily thought about the information her aunt had given her. She tried to come up with questions whose answers could add to what she knew.

"You said one of our horses was tied to the hitching post at the shop," Lily said, running her finger around the rim of the coffee cup. She looked up and asked, "Do you know which one? I know we have, or at least *had*, quite a few horses when Violet and I went to England. But would you happen to remember which one you saw?"

Ida May looked at Lily, sighed, and replied, "I'm sure it was Lightnin', dear."

"My horse?" Lily asked, surprised. "Well, I suppose since I was not here Papa used Lightnin' and my cart."

"The cart was not at the shop," Ida May said reluctantly.

"It wasn't?" Lily asked. "Well, I suppose Papa had been riding him."

Ida May cleared her throat and said slowly, "I'm afraid, dear, there was no saddle there either."

Lily quickly looked her aunt straight in the eyes and asked,

"Aunt Ida May, what are you trying to tell me? There's something you haven't told me yet."

"The sheriff tried to say later that Lightnin' was the horse that killed your father," Ida May said. "But I made it quite clear that Lightnin' was tied to the hitching post when I found Charlie, and since I was the first one there, I said there was no way Lightnin' could have done it."

"Oh, no, Aunt Ida May," Lily said with a quick intake of breath. "Lightnin' is as tame as a kitten. He would never harm anyone, especially Papa or one of us."

"That's what I said, too," Ida May replied. "And I asked the sheriff how he could say a horse did it when there was no sign of another horse anywhere. And he said maybe someone found Charlie before I did and just tied up Lightnin' and left."

Lily stood up and quickly walked around the room. She stopped and said in an angry voice, "I need to talk to the sheriff myself and tell him a thing or two. And to demand that he investigate the matter thoroughly, and I mean *thoroughly*." She came back to her chair and took a deep swallow of the hot coffee.

"I tried to get him to look into things, dear, and he just flat refused," Ida May said. "Maybe he'll listen to you."

"I'll go up to see him tomorrow, now that you are here and I won't have to take Violet with me," Lily said.

"I don't think you should go off that far by yourself, Lily," Aunt Ida May objected. "It's a good little ride to Greenville and back."

"Well, his office is there and that's where I'll have to go," Lily said. She had a sudden idea. "Maybe Logan would go with me."

"I'm sure he would," Ida May said.

"I want to talk to Logan anyway, about everything," Lily said. "He said he'd be back tomorrow, so maybe he'll come early enough for us to go and get back before dark."

"Lily, sometimes the sheriff is hard to find. He covers the whole Greenville County, you know, and he doesn't always stay in his office," her aunt reminded her. "It was nearly dark that day before he came to talk to us, Janie Belle and me, that is, and of course things had to be taken care of before he got here. Logan arranged for your father to . . . be taken into town."

"So he didn't actually see . . . what you had found," Lily remarked.

"No, he didn't," Ida May said. "He just asked questions and made his own decision about what happened. And that's one reason he should have made an investigation."

Lily's thoughts roamed and she asked, "Aunt Ida May, did you see Papa the day before? I'd like to know how he was feeling and how things were, with me gone to England and him here alone."

"Well, yes, the day before was Sunday, and your father came home with Janie Belle and me from church and had dinner with us," Ida May explained. "He didn't stay long. He said he needed to see Logan about something."

"About something?" Lily asked.

"Yes, something about picking out some timber to be cut on the back of your land," Ida May explained. "Logan had help coming in the next morning to start plowing and sowing the wheat."

"Did Papa look all right? Did he say anything about Violet and me?" Lily asked, anxiously waiting for the reply.

"Why, he looked just fine, like always," Ida May said. "And he did say he hoped to get straightened out enough with bills by next spring so he could get y'all back home again." Ida May looked at Lily and added softly, "He did miss y'all terribly bad."

Tears sprang into Lily's eyes. "If only we had not gone to England," she said in a shaky voice. "And you know, Aunt Ida May, I almost lost Violet on the trip going over. She got awfully sick and if it hadn't been for a rich lady on the ship who got Violet into the infirmary with a doctor she might not have recovered."

"Oh, dear, what happened?" Ida May asked anxiously. "Why didn't you write and let us know when you got to England? We got letters from you but you never mentioned this."

"I didn't want to worry Papa," Lily said. "Violet did recover and I planned to tell him about it when we returned home."

"I'm sorry, child," her aunt said, reaching for Lily's hand. "You've had so many burdens to bear, and at such a young age, too. First, your mother ill and helpless all those years when you should have been growing up as other children do, then this with Violet, and of course with your Papa, and now you are left on your own."

"No, no, Aunt Ida May," Lily argued tearfully. "My mother was not a burden. I loved her so much I would have spent the rest of my life caring for her if she had only lived."

"Well, I'm here to help in any way you need me," her aunt said. "And I don't know if you've thought of this yet, but we need to get Violet enrolled in school."

"Oh, definitely," Lily said, blinking away the tears and pushing back stray blonde tendrils. "I've already told her she'll have to go to school, but she's not very interested in it. I may have trouble with her about that."

"I'll go with you whenever you get ready to see Miss Potter," Aunt Ida May offered.

"Who is Miss Potter?" Lily asked.

"Oh, you've been gone so long you don't know that your old teacher, Miss Bagwell, finally retired. Miss Potter came down from North Carolina and was accepted for the job," Ida May explained. "She's young, awfully pretty, and probably won't stay long here in the country, but I understand the children love her."

"Things sure do change fast, don't they?" Lily said. "I always figured Miss Bagwell would stay until she got so old she'd just plain drop dead." She laughed.

"No, she went home to her mother in Charleston. I understand she was up in her years and was no longer able to take care of herself, so Miss Bagwell went to stay with her," Ida May explained.

"I suppose I should get Violet started in school as soon as possible," Lily said. "It'll take her mind off other things and she'll probably make friends and get interested."

"It's too bad there aren't any children close enough to be neighbors," Aunt Ida May said. "You know, I've always thought

Ossie should have married again and had a family. He loves Violet so much."

Lily said with a smile, "And Violet thinks he's her big brother, or something." Her smile faded and she changed the subject. "I'll be glad when Ossie gets home and I can talk things over with him."

"It was lucky he was on the same ship with you, wasn't it?" Ida May said as she sipped her coffee.

"Definitely," Lily agreed. "You know we had some strange things going on during our journey."

Lily told Ida May about Wilbur and his two friends. "Have you heard of these people named Whitaker that have moved to Fountain Inn?"

"No, I haven't," Ida May replied. "And we usually know everything that's going on around this part of the country. I can't imagine why we haven't learned about these newcomers. What do they do for a living?"

"I don't know," Lily replied. "I never was able to find out. Wilbur just said his family had money and he really didn't have to work. That was all I could get out of him."

"Maybe Logan has heard of them, or Roy," Ida May said. "But if they're so rich, I don't imagine our paths will ever cross."

"Oh, Wilbur at one point asked if he could come calling on me when I got home but I hope I never meet up with him again," Lily said. "He was a strange fellow, and probably dangerous, too—at least in Ossie's opinion."

"After what you've told me about his friend being found overboard and all, I'd agree with Ossie," Ida May said.

"I hope I hear from the captain so I'll know what happened. The captain said he might get in touch with me later," Lily said. She stood up and added, "I need to see what Violet is doing. I don't see her out there." She walked to the doorway and looked outside.

Violet was sitting in the grass with the puppy asleep in her lap. She was gently rubbing the fur on his head. When she looked up and saw Lily watching, she quickly put her finger to her lips and said in a loud whisper, "Sh-h-h-h! He's asleep."

Lily smiled and called to her, "Not anymore." The puppy had seen Lily and jumped out of Violet's lap to run to her. Violet followed and snatched him up when he reached Lily.

"He's hungry," Violet told Lily. "That's why he woke up. Is it time to eat supper?"

"It's getting close to time to start preparing it," Lily said.

Violet turned to go back into the yard, carrying the puppy with her. "I guess we'll just have to wait then," she mumbled to the animal.

"It won't be long," Lily called to her, and then went back into the kitchen where Ida May had taken their cups to the sink.

"The child is hungry," Ida May said. "Now let's see what we can find to fix for supper." She opened the door to the pantry.

"Just anything will do," Lily said, following her.

"That's no way to live," Ida May told her. "It's too late in the day now but bright and early in the morning I'll prepare some decent food. Maybe bake a hen if Logan will bring us one and cook a big pot of beans with potatoes."

"You are really making me hungry," Lily said with a little laugh as they examined the stock in the pantry. "The food in England just doesn't taste right and it'll sure be good to get some real home-cooked meals."

"Well, while you are gone to town tomorrow I'll get something going," her aunt said.

That brought Lily's mind back to the reason for going to town. She was anxious to talk to the sheriff and she hoped Logan would come by in time to go with her. There were lots of questions she wanted to ask of him as well.

Later that night, after a hearty meal, Lily was able to get Violet into her own bed by allowing the puppy to sleep in a box in the child's room. The arrangement was only for that night, but Lily was worried about what would happen on future days when she insisted the puppy stay downstairs in the crate.

Lily and Aunt Ida May were both tired and went to their rooms. Lily got ready for bed and crawled between the covers.

She had so much on her mind she couldn't sleep. She tossed and turned for hours and finally got up, put on a robe, and roamed through the house. She ended up in the big leather chair in her father's office. Reaching for a quilt that her mother had made years ago, one that her father had hung over the back of a straight chair in the corner, Lily pulled her mother's quilt around her and curled up in her father's chair.

She finally drifted off to sleep.

Chapter Ten
The Blacksmith Shop

The sunshine coming through the window and onto Lily's face woke her the next morning. She straightened up, looked around the room, and said to herself, "I didn't sleep in my bed."

She stood up, stretched to get the kinks out from having slept in the chair, and hurried to her bedroom to get dressed. As she passed the room Ida May was occupying she noticed the door was open. She looked inside and saw the bed was already made up. So Aunt Ida May must be downstairs already.

Glancing inside Violet's room, she found her missing, too. And here she had meant to be up bright and early, but she was evidently the last one to wake.

After hurriedly putting on a blue calico dress, Lily brushed her long hair, pinned it up, and quickly buttoned her shoes. She rushed downstairs to find the other two.

Aunt Ida May was busy in the kitchen, frying bacon, making coffee, and stirring a pot that Lily knew must contain grits. Her aunt never ate breakfast without grits.

"Why didn't you wake me, Aunt Ida May?" Lily asked as she walked over to the stove.

"Well, I looked in your room and you weren't there, so I assumed you had come down here. But then you weren't here either," Ida May told her, pushing back a wisp of dark hair. "Violet was awake and she dressed and brought the puppy down to the yard. I told her to go look for you, and she came back and said you were asleep in your father's office. I told her to just let you sleep until I got breakfast done. You needed the rest."

"Aunt Ida May, I'm sorry. I should have been down here at least helping," Lily told her aunt with a little smile of affection. She went to the china cupboard and took out dishes to set the table. "Is Violet still outside?"

"Why, yes, she's playing with that puppy and that puppy is the best thing that could have happened to her," the woman said as she turned the bacon in the iron frying pan.

"I agree," Lily said, setting the dishes on the table. "Maybe she'll stay involved with the puppy until a little time has passed and things are not so fresh." She looked down at the number of dishes she had set out. There were three plates and three cups and saucers, like always. Aunt Ida May was filling in the gap.

Violet suddenly appeared in the open doorway and excitedly called to Lily, "Logan just brought some chickens and put them in the pen and I think he's hungry."

Lily looked at her and smiled. Ida May asked, "Now how do you know he's hungry?"

" 'Cause he said he could smell that bacon a mile away," Violet said, and ran back out into the yard.

Lily walked over and looked outside. Logan was coming up the pathway from the chicken pen. "Good morning," she called to him. "Aunt Ida May has breakfast just about done. Come on in and eat with us."

"Lawsy mercy, that's the best invite I've had in a long time," Logan said as he came through the doorway and into the kitchen. "I knew if I got here early enough, Miss Ida May would be cooking up sumpin' good."

Ida May glanced at him and smiled as she put a lid on the pot of grits and set them off the burner. "If you're all that hungry, just wash your hands over there and we'll be sitting down any minute now," she said as she picked up the cooking fork and removed the bacon from the frying pan to a large platter.

"And I'll just get more dishes," Lily said as she took another plate and a cup and saucer from the cupboard and brought them to the table.

Logan washed up at the sink and dried his hands on the towel hanging on a hook.

"What are you planning on doing today, Logan?" Lily asked as she helped Ida May place the food on the table.

"Well, I've still got the crew working on that timber on the back line," Logan said as he looked at her. "And they're men I can trust to get the work done, so if you're thinking of something you need me for I'd be glad to oblige."

Violet came in, bringing the puppy with her, and dropped him into the crate by the stove. She climbed up on the stool at the sink and washed up.

Lily looked at the child, then back at Logan, and said, "I'd like to go to Greenville today, and I'd appreciate it a lot if you could go with me."

Logan looked at her in surprise and asked, "To Greenville? What do you be needin' in Greenville?"

Lily looked at him and nodded in Violet's direction as she replied, "There's someone I'd like to see up there. I want to ask some questions."

Logan instantly understood that she didn't want Violet to hear. "If I was you I wouldn't go up there jes' yet," he said. "I'd talk to people around here first."

Lily shook her head and said, "I do want to talk to you—later when we're alone, but I intend complaining in a big way about why no investigation has been made."

"Well, if you feel that away 'bout it," Logan said. "I'll be glad to go with you. I'll jes' run over and let the men know where I am going first."

"Well now, first of all, we're going to eat this food while it's hot," Ida May told him. "Now let's all get busy with it."

They sat down to the table and Lily looked across at Ida May. "Would you return thanks, Aunt Ida May?"

"Of course, child," her aunt replied, and as soon as she had done so, Violet began eagerly asking for some of everything.

When they had finished, Logan left to talk to his men with the promise that he would harness up the cart and bring it on his way back. Violet took the puppy outside.

Ida May went in the pantry and came back out with a small covered basket. She took it to the stove and set it on the cook table nearby. "I figured you'd need something to eat since that's a long trip up there and back so I made enough biscuits and cooked sausage here to do y'all till you get back," she said as she began dropping the meat into a fruit jar.

"Thank you," Lily said as she continued clearing the table. "I didn't even think of food."

"And since Logan brought some chickens I'll have one cooked for supper when y'all get back," Ida May said as she filled the basket. "Now you go get yourself freshened up and I'll finish here in the kitchen, so you'll be ready when Logan gets back, and so you won't be gone so late if you get started now."

"Thank you for helping me, Aunt Ida May, and you're right," Lily said as she straightened up to untie the apron she had put on. She hung it on a hook by the pantry door. "I'll be back down by the time Logan gets back." She hurried upstairs to look for a shawl to take in case the day turned out to be chilly. Opening the drawer in her bureau she found the shawl on top of everything. As she held it up, she realized it was black and she should be in mourning for her father. Aunt Ida May wore black all the time, so she had not even thought about this.

"Oh, Papa!" she moaned to herself as she quickly rummaged through the tall wardrobe in her room. She took down the black dress she had worn when her mother died and, quickly slipping out of the calico she was wearing, she pulled it on and fastened the tiny black buttons.

Without even looking in the mirror, for fear the tears would start again if she viewed the dress of mourning, she snatched up the black shawl, threw it around her shoulders, and put on the black hat that went with the dress.

Lily went down to the kitchen where Ida May was just throwing out the dishwater. Her aunt looked at her and said, "You look nice, Lily, but do you think your father would want you to wear all that black? You know he always liked bright colors, especially on you and Violet."

Lily looked down at her dress, and her eyes clouded. "I know, but I thought I should wear this to town, and I just don't know about later."

"Remember he had you hang up those clothes not long after you lost your mother and wouldn't let you take them to England," Ida May reminded her.

"I know, I know," Lily said in a quavering voice. "I'll think about it later, after I get back from town." She straightened her shoulders, cleared her throat, and asked, "Are you sure you don't mind if I go off and leave you with Violet and everything for the day? I'm not sure how long I'll be gone."

"Oh, hush, child," Ida May said, wiping her hands on the apron she wore. "You just get this journey over with and don't worry about me."

Without a word, Lily rushed over to her aunt, squeezed her tight, and kissed her cheek. Ida May returned the embrace. Then she reached back and handed Lily the filled picnic basket that was sitting on the table.

"I'm ready any time you are," Logan called from the open doorway.

"I'm all set to go," Lily said, quickly joining him.

Violet was standing in the walkway with the puppy when she saw Lily leaving with Logan. She waved and said, "Bye, Lily, we're going to have a good time while you're gone."

"I hope so, dear. You mind Aunt Ida May now and don't give her any trouble, you hear?" Lily called to her as she stepped up into the waiting cart.

"Yes, ma'am," Violet called back, and this time she waved the puppy's foot to Lily and Logan as he drove the cart down the driveway.

Lily began getting her thoughts in order to talk to Logan. When they reached the main road, she asked, "Would you mind if we detoured by the blacksmith shop? I . . . haven't . . . been there yet."

"Of course, Miss Lily," Logan replied as he drove on.

Lily looked at Logan, smiled slightly, and said, "Logan, you know I'd much rather you just call me Lily, like you always did."

Logan glanced at her and explained, "Well, now that you own all this property and I work for you and all I thought it'd be more fittin' if I jes' added the 'miss' to show my respect."

"Oh, Logan, you've known me all my life. You lived here on the land before I was ever born when you worked for my grandfather. In fact, I consider you part of the family," Lily said. "I call you Logan. I always have, so why should you put that 'miss' in front of my name?"

"Well, if you insist," Logan finally agreed.

Lily's thoughts became sad as the road to the blacksmith shop came into view. "And, Logan, please tell me everything you know about . . . that day, please," Lily said as he turned the cart down the road. Ahead was her father's blacksmith shop and this was probably the first time in her life she had ever gone down this road without her father being at the end of it.

She glanced at Logan, whose face was covered with pain. He didn't reply for a few moments, but stopped the cart by the building and helped Lily down.

"It was right there," Logan explained as he pointed to a place on the ground near the furnace. "He was lying right there." His old voice trembled.

Lily ran to stoop down and sift the dirt on the spot through her fingers. Tears dripped onto her black dress.

Logan shuffled his feet and continued. "I was working the back timber and had to go up the road to get another axe from the barn. One of the men had split the handle on his axe."

Lily pulled a handkerchief out of her pocket and stood up on shaky legs. As she dried her face, she said, "Aunt Ida May told me you found her down here."

"That's right," Logan said. "I heard somebody screaming at the top of their lungs and looked down from the main road and saw someone down here. When I came on down, I found Miss Ida May hysterical. She couldn't even utter a word she was so distraught. Then I looked down there and saw . . . the reason."

Lily tried to steady her voice as she asked, "Logan, do you think a horse did it?"

"No way!" Logan said emphatically. He began to walk around the shop and said, "Couldn't have been a horse."

Lily followed and ran her hand over the edge of the cold furnace and looked down at the bellows lying beside it. She turned to the anvil and found a horseshoe and a hammer on top. Horseshoe nails were strewn about the surrounding ground. The crowbar for removing old horseshoes was lying there and the iron tongs her father had used to handle the hot metal.

Logan said in a soft voice, "It's all jes' like I found it. Nothing's been disturbed. I jes' didn't know what to do about it, and your aunts said jes' leave it alone for the time being, so I did."

"Yes, let's just leave it like my papa left it," Lily said in a whisper.

Suddenly there was a loud whinny from Lightnin', and Lily looked back at him standing by the cart in the roadway. The horse made the noise again and chills ran over Lily because it sounded like a cry of anguish. She ran to him and Logan followed.

Patting the animal's head, she whispered, "I know, it hurts to come here. You were here and saw it all." Lightnin' nuzzled her hand and calmed down. Lily looked at Logan and said, "I think we'd better go."

"Yes," Logan agreed, and he helped her up into the cart.

Without a word, he turned the vehicle toward the main road and they continued on their journey in silence until Lily finally spoke.

"I suppose you understood that I'm going to see the sheriff. I couldn't make myself clear this morning in front of Violet."

"I understood all right, and I knew you'd be doin' that very thing soon as you got home, and I'm with you all the way on this. I've not been able to get anything done but maybe you can," Logan replied.

"I won't rest until something is done," Lily said determinedly. She held her hat against the breeze as they traveled on. She looked at the old man beside her and asked, "Logan, why do you think Lightnin' was upset back there at the shop?"

"He probably saw and heard everything that happened and, even though he's a horse, you know what a big pet he is. Many a time I've seen him rub his head against your papa, wanting to be petted," Logan said. "He's mourning in his own way."

Lily swallowed hard. Logan was right. Lightnin' missed her father.

When they reached the courthouse in Greenville, Logan tied up the horse and cart in the yard and helped Lily down.

"I want you to come in with me, Logan, please," she said, looking up at the old man as she shook down her long skirts and adjusted her hat.

"Of course I'm coming with you," Logan said. "I have my own complaint to make, even though I've made it before and it didn't do any good."

"Thank you, Logan," Lily said, and reaching for his old wrinkled hand, she walked with him to the door.

Lily had never been to this place before, but Logan knew exactly where to find the sheriff's offices. At the end of a long corridor he opened a door that had glass in it with lettering reading, "John Meadows, Sheriff of Greenville County."

As she entered the room Lily saw there was no one there. A long table strewn with papers was at one end. An old desk stood at the other side, with several cane-bottomed chairs between. At the back was a closed door. Logan went straight to that door, tapped on it, and without waiting to get an answer from inside he pushed it open and stepped into another room.

"There's no one here either," Lily said with disappointment. She looked around at the desk in one corner, two chairs, and a small cabinet with a padlock on it.

"I'll find out where he is. There ought to be at least a deputy here," Logan said as he led the way back through the other room and into the hallway. "You jes' sit right there on that bench and I'll be right back," he told her.

Lily sat down on the long bench running almost the length of the corridor and waited as she watched Logan disappear around the corner.

The old man was back in a few minutes, shaking his head as he told her, "Seems there was an accident over near Pickens County and the sheriff and both his deputies have gone over there. I talked to the law clerk and told him to give the sheriff the message that you wanted to talk to him right away."

Lily stood up with a sigh and said, "I suppose he'll be gone a long time."

"Well, yes, probably," Logan agreed.

"Since we're already here, let's just walk around and maybe go see some of the stores. We can check back after a while to see if he's returned," Lily suggested.

Lily had never had a chance to walk down Main Street in Greenville. She stopped to look at merchandise through plate glass windows as they passed a large hardware store, a harness shop, and several stores selling household goods. There were stables and a carriage factory, and finally they came to where Reedy River crossed the street. Going back up on the other side of the street she spotted a sign hanging over the sidewalk.

"Look! That sign says 'Red Hot Racket.' Let's see what they sell," she said.

"I believe it's a dry goods store," Logan said, smiling down at her.

When they walked through the doorway Lily could see that Logan was right, but there was a lot of other merchandise, too. The store sold everything from washtubs to cheap jewelry. She roamed the aisles on the creaky wooden floor and examined the goods displayed on every counter. Ending up at the dry goods section, she looked at the beautiful material stacked there—satin, silk, and voile among the staples of cotton and muslin fabrics.

"Oh, what I could do with this!" Lily exclaimed as she removed her gloves and fingered a bolt of bright blue silk. "This would make a beautiful dress for Violet."

"Well, I believe your father had an account here," Logan told her. "You could inquire."

Lily quickly looked at Logan and asked, "Do you think we could afford it? I don't know a thing about Papa's finances, and you know I've got to settle down and learn the business."

Logan scratched his grey head and said, "I jes' don't imagine that little piece of material would cost very much anyway. Why don't you ask about chargin' it and you can get into your father's records when you get home?"

Lily loved beautiful material and enjoyed making it into beautiful garments. Now that she would have so much time on her hands, with Violet in school most of the day, she would be able to sew. She hesitated about buying the silk though.

"I do know the timber we're taking off the back of the land will bring quite a sum. Your father told me that," Logan explained.

"Well, I'll take a chance then on this one thing," Lily said as she continued holding the blue silk.

A clerk, in what appeared to be his Sunday clothes, came to her side and asked, "May I help you, please, ma'am?"

"I'm Lily Masterson, Charlie Masterson's daughter, and I—" she hesitated as she saw the man take a quick breath in surprise.

"Yes, ma'am, yes, ma'am, I'm terribly sorry about your papa," he told her. "Now you want to put this silk on his account? That'll be fine. How much do you need?" He seemed anxious that she take the material.

Lily couldn't understand the man's attitude, and she glanced up at Logan who was standing nearby, hoping he might make more sense of the awkward situation.

"Tell him how much it takes to make Violet a dress," Logan said as he raised his eyebrows.

Lily looked back at the clerk and gave him the amount she needed. "I am sure four yards will be plenty, since it's narrow width," she said.

"And what else, ma'am?" the clerk said as he lifted the bolt.

"Nothing else, right now," Lily quickly told him.

He carried the bolt to the counter to measure off the material. As he was cutting it, he said, "Miss Masterson, I'd just like to say your father had plenty of credit here and he always paid on time. If there's anything else at all, I'd be glad to wrap it up for you."

"Thank you, I appreciate that, but that's all right now," Lily said, and she again looked at Logan who was listening and watching the transaction.

Once the man had wrapped the material and Lily had signed the book for it, she and Logan started to leave the store. She glanced across the large room and suddenly saw Thomas Hickman and Wilbur Whitaker make a quick exit out the door as they caught her look.

Lily quickly grabbed Logan's hand to stop him and said, "I just saw the two men from the ship, Wilbur Whitaker and his friend Thomas Hickman, go out the door. They were here in this store."

"Who?" Logan asked as he looked at the front door.

"The men from the ship that I told you about. The two the captain was asking questions about," Lily explained. "Oh, well, they're gone now."

"This is a big town, no telling who you might see," Logan said as he reached to open the door.

"You're right," Lily agreed. They stepped outside onto the sidewalk and she said, "I'd like to check one more time to see if the sheriff is in before we leave town."

"Fine," Logan agreed.

They went back to the courthouse, but the lawmen had still not returned. Logan left another message with the law clerk, but Lily had to give up for the day because it was a long way home and they would have to leave now.

As they stepped into the cart, Lily noticed the picnic basket in the back and said, "We haven't even eaten yet. You must be hungry. I just plumb forgot about it."

"Let's get out of this town and pull off under a tree down the road and see what Miss Ida May put in that basket," Logan said as he started Lightnin' on his way.

When Logan found a place to stop, Lily realized she was hungry. It didn't take long to consume every morsel in the basket.

The fall days were beginning to shorten, but they got home before dark, just in time for supper, and Ida May had the meal waiting.

Lily was disappointed that she had not been able to talk with the sheriff, but she hoped he would come out to see her. And if he didn't in a few days, she'd go right back to his office. Sooner or later she was going to catch up with the man.

And that night as she lay awake thinking about the journey to Greenville, she wondered why Wilbur and Thomas had quickly avoided her. Evidently, Thomas must also live somewhere nearby.

Chapter Eleven
Fire!

Lily was up at the crack of dawn the next morning. She had lots of things on her mind that had kept her awake most of the night. After quickly making up her bed, she glanced at the black dress she had hung up the night before, and then took down a gingham dress. She put it on and went down to the kitchen.

She got the fire going in the big iron cookstove and set the coffeepot on it to percolate. By that time Violet appeared in the doorway with the puppy.

"Take him outside, hurry," Lily told the child. "We can't have him messing up the floor."

Violet ran, opened the back door, and went outside with the dog. She set the little animal down in the grass and flopped down beside him. Lily watched through the open doorway, then turned back inside to prepare breakfast.

While she was getting supplies from the pantry, Ida May came into the room. "Good morning," Ida May greeted her. "I hope you slept well last night, child."

"I slept some, but I had so much to think about it kept me wide awake till way in the night sometime," Lily said. "I hope you had a good night's rest." She carried the can of grits and a bowl of eggs to the cook table.

"Yes, I feel right sprite this morning," Ida May said as she helped prepare the food.

It didn't take them long to get the meal on the table, and as soon as they had finished eating, Violet went back outside with the puppy. Lily and Ida May cleared the table.

As they worked together, Lily discussed her problems. "I know I need to look at Papa's books and papers so I can get some idea of what is being done on the farm here and how we stand with money," Lily said as she gathered up the tablecloth and took it to the door to shake it out.

"Yes, you're going to have to do something about business," Ida May agreed. She hung the pots on hooks behind the stove. "Since Logan can't read or write too well, somebody's going to have to do it."

Lily brought the tablecloth back and spread it on the table. She straightened up to look at her aunt. "I suppose the first thing I need to do, I should go visit Papa's grave." Her voice trembled.

"Yes, dear, he's buried there beside your mother in Fairview Cemetery," her aunt said. "But I want to let you know ahead of time. There's only a temporary marker on his grave. We were waiting for you to come home to pick out the tombstone."

"Then that's another thing I need to do," Lily said as she took off the apron she was wearing. "I wish Ossie would hurry up and come home so I could talk to him about things. I know Logan is capable of overseeing the work, but I'll have to take care of the business part and I don't know anything about it at all."

"Neither do I, child," Ida May replied. "I've always said it's good Janie Belle married your Uncle Aaron, because she doesn't know a thing about it either. Course, he's getting up in years now and he's cut back on a lot of the farming."

"If you don't mind watching Violet for me I think I'll go over to the cemetery now. I want to get back just in case that sheriff comes by later," Lily said.

"Of course, dear, go right ahead," Ida May replied. "Just don't stay gone too long or I'll be worried about you."

"I won't," Lily said. "I'll get a hat and take the cart."

After she got the hat, Lily went down to the barn. Lightnin' came up to the fence when he saw her.

"We're going out, Lightnin'," she told him. She opened the gate and led him out.

As she hitched the horse to the cart, she was thankful her father had taught her how to do that. When he had given Lightnin' to her several years ago, he had told her she would have to take care of him in every way, and she eagerly learned.

Lily drove the cart up the pathway from the barn and stopped to speak to Violet. "You stay right around the yard now where Aunt Ida May can see you," she said. "I'll be back in a little while."

"I want to go, too," Violet whined as she set the puppy down in the grass.

"Not this time. I'll take you next time I have to go out," Lily told her.

"When?" Violet asked eagerly.

"I'm not sure right now, but it'll be soon. Be a good girl now for Aunt Ida May. I love you," Lily said as she threw a kiss to the child.

"I love you," Violet said, blowing a kiss back.

As Lily drove on, she realized this first visit to the cemetery might prove to be too unsettling for her, so she thought it best not to bring Violet along. But sooner or later she would have to take her little sister to see the grave.

When she got to the churchyard she stopped the cart, stepped down, and tied the reins to a hitching post under a tree. She glanced up at the white wooden church where generations of her family had worshipped. No one was around.

Walking slowly to the big iron gate to the cemetery, she paused and then pushed it open. Taking a deep breath, she made her way down the center pathway to the family plot. She stared at the mound of dirt that still looked fresh and the small wooden cross at the head. Kneeling down, she read her father's name, and then the tears came.

After a while, she stood up and looked at her mother's grave. Her monument had been put up before Lily and Violet went to

England. She read her mother's name and fresh tears wet her face.

"Mama! Papa!" she cried to herself as she stood there, helpless and lonely.

Finally, wiping her eyes, she heard Lightnin' whinny on the other side of the rock wall. She walked quickly up the pathway to see what was bothering him. When she got to the gate, she saw a man on horseback riding out of the churchyard into the road. Lightnin' was stomping his feet.

With her eye on the rider, she hurried to her horse. The man glanced back. It was Thomas Hickman! He galloped his horse down the road and was soon out of sight.

Lily rubbed Lightnin's head and said, "Now, I wonder what he was doing here. Calm down, Lightnin'. We're going home."

As soon as the horse had quieted down, Lily picked up the reins, stepped up into the cart, and headed home. She drove slowly, thinking about her father and his death. The more she thought about it, the more she was certain someone had taken him from her and she wouldn't rest until she found out who was responsible.

As she turned into the main road toward home, Lily happened to glance over distant fields and was alarmed to see smoke rising in the distance. If she was not mistaken, it was in the direction of her home.

"Lightnin', let's go!" she called to her horse as she shook the reins.

The animal picked up on her urgency and broke into a run. The cart bounced over the rough dirt road and almost unseated Lily, but she clung to the bar on the side of the seat with one hand and held the reins in the other as she lifted her face toward heaven and prayed.

"Dear Lord, please don't let it be my house!" she cried. "Please!"

Lightnin' didn't need any guidance from Lily. He headed straight home. As they came around the last bend in the road and the smoke got thicker, Lily could see it was her barn on fire. "Thank you, Lord!" she cried. Her home was not burning.

Lightnin' balked on the road to the house, so she brought him to a stop, threw the reins around a limb, and lifting her long skirts, ran the rest of the way.

"Violet! Aunt Ida May! Where are you?" she cried as she hurried toward the house.

"Here, Lily, don't go too close to the barn. The men are working on the fire," Aunt Ida May called to her from the yard. She was holding Violet's hand and they were watching the flames shoot from the roof of the barn.

Lily saw they were safe, and disregarding her aunt's orders she kept running until she reached the men. She realized there were several dozen men working, trying to save her barn, but she also realized the roof was already badly burned and was ready to collapse. Tears came into her smoke-filled eyes as she remembered how proud her father had been when he built the barn just a few years ago. And now it was being destroyed.

But what caused it?

As she tried to distinguish who was who in the thick smoke, she spotted Logan just as he saw her. He quickly came to meet her.

"Don't get so close," he warned her. "It's ready to fall, and the burning timber may fly everywhere. Get back up in the yard." His voice was firm.

"Oh, Logan, what happened?" she cried as she moved only a few feet back. "Tell me what happened?"

"I'll talk to you later. Now get back all the way to the house, right now," Logan told her in a loud voice.

Lily knew there was nothing she could do, so she moved backward, toward the house, until she had reached Ida May and Violet in the yard. She kept her eyes glued to the burning barn.

"Thank goodness Logan had taken the livestock to his house at the other end of the property, so no animals were inside or in the fenced area," Ida May told her. She held a handkerchief to her nose. "Logan put the chickens in Ossie's chicken pen."

"What happened? What happened? Please tell me!" Lily demanded.

"We don't know yet," Ida May said. "Not long after you left,

Violet had the puppy in the yard here. She came into the house for a drink of water, and when she went back outside the puppy was gone. I helped her look for it, and when we went toward the barn the puppy came running up the pathway." She paused to wipe her soot-covered face.

"What did that have to do with the barn burning?" Lily asked.

"Well, when we got that close, I thought I smelled something burning, and when I looked inside, the loft was on fire," Ida May explained. "It just happened that Roy was in Ossie's barn over there and not somewhere out in the fields, and he heard me scream for help and came running."

"It happened so fast!" Lily said as she stared at the burning building.

"Roy jumped on a horse and spread the word, and within a few minutes most of the men in the whole countryside were here trying to put it out," Ida May said. "And he got Logan and his men from the backside of the land where they were cutting timber."

"I'd like to know what caused it," Lily said. As she spoke, a heavy rain suddenly fell and drenched them. She looked up at the sky through the smoke because she didn't remember seeing any clouds before. But now the rain was coming down in torrents. "Thank you, dear Lord!" she cried as Ida May and Violet ran for cover on the back porch of the house.

Lily stood there dripping wet and watched the flames gradually die. The rain-soaked men kept working. Since the roof was practically burned off, the rain could come down through it and extinguish the flames on the inside.

Finally, the fire died. The men walked back in groups and talked. Lily saw Logan in the crowd and she hurried to speak to him. He looked down at her and shook his wet, dirty head.

"The roof didn't collapse," was all Lily could think of to say.

"No, but it's in dangerous shape, so don't go near the building," Logan told her. "In all my years I've seen lots of fires, but I've jes' never exactly seen one that the good Lord put out. The sun was shinin', and suddenly the rain came pourin' down."

"And look!" Lily said. "Now the sun is coming back out." She gazed upward through the smoky haze left by the fire. "The Lord does miraculous things."

The sunshine came through.

"I'll be back to talk to you later, but right now we've got to clean up around here and be sure there is not even a tiny fire anywhere. Now, I know how headstrong you can be sometimes, but your father made me the foreman here, and I'm acting as foreman, and ordering you to stay away from the barn. Understand?"

Lily looked up at the old man, knowing he was thinking of her safety. "I understand, Logan," she said. "I won't go near it until you tell me I can."

Roy walked up to them and told Lily, "I'll get Lightnin' and the cart for you and put them inside Ossie's fence until we get all this cleaned up and safe again."

"Thank you, Roy," Lily told him. She glanced down at her soggy skirts and said, "And I need cleaning up myself. Logan, you and Roy come eat with us. It must be almost noontime, and I'm sure Aunt Ida May has something prepared."

The dirty men looked at their own clothes, then at each other, and laughed.

"When I get cleaned up myself, I'll come over," Roy promised as he walked on toward Lightnin', who was still tied to the tree limb.

"That goes for me, too," Logan told her. He went back down the pathway to join the men at the barn.

Lily's wet skirts were heavy but she hurried toward the house. As she entered the back door into the kitchen, Ida May was stirring something in a big pot on the stove. It smelled delicious. Violet was sitting on the floor, playing with the puppy.

Ida May turned to look at Lily and said, "You hurry and get cleaned up now. This vegetable soup is almost done, and I've got cornbread in the oven to go with it. And Logan brought over some buttermilk this morning."

"It sounds wonderful," Lily said, looking at her aunt and then at Violet. "Why didn't y'all get all wet and dirty like I did?" She pushed back her wet hair.

"Because we didn't get close enough to the fire to get covered with soot, and we got on the porch when it rained. Now, get going and hurry up," Ida May said. "I've made enough for Logan, too, and I suppose Roy will be eating with us, and whoever else wants to. I've got plenty."

"I'll sure hurry," Lily said. She rushed to her room to remove the wet, dirty clothes.

Quickly grabbing a dress from the wardrobe and undergarments from the bureau drawer, she hurried into the upstairs bathroom that her father had had installed for her mother. Even though they had electricity in their house, they only used the power to pump water. Her father had not got around to wiring for lights.

As she bathed and washed her hair, she thought about the fire in the barn. She had gone in there herself that morning to get the cart, and she hadn't smelled or noticed anything out of the ordinary. How had it happened so fast? Someone must have set it, and that someone must have been in there when she was. Chills ran over her at the thought. But why would anyone want to burn down their barn?

In a few minutes, she was back downstairs in the kitchen, and Logan and Roy, both cleaned up enough to be presentable, came in the back door.

"Sure is nice of y'all to ask me to help eat all this good-smelling food," Roy said with a big smile. He reached and gave the puppy a pat just before Violet put the animal in the crate.

"Sure is nice of y'all to help out with the barn," Lily told him as Ida May waved everyone to a seat at the table.

"We'll have to order out the lumber and get it repaired jes' as soon as we can, because it'll be getting cold purty soon," Logan said, sitting down next to Violet at the table.

"Oh, goodness, that means money. I haven't looked into Papa's records yet to see how his finances stand," Lily said, motioning Roy to the other side of the table.

Ida May filled bowls with the steaming soup, and Lily carried them to the table. She pulled the long pan of cornbread out of the oven, sliced it quickly, and Lily placed that before the men. Then, going to the jug of buttermilk by the sink, Lily filled glasses and passed them around. To Lily this was a good country meal, and she realized she was hungry.

They discussed the fire while they ate, and Lily decided this was another matter for the sheriff.

"When that sheriff comes out here, I want to talk to him about this fire, too," Lily said to her aunt. Then she looked at Logan and asked, "Is there any way we could get word to him to come out and look at the barn?"

"Well, yes, we'll probably have to go into Greenville to order the lumber, so we could just go by and see him while we're there," Logan said between bites of cornbread.

"If you'll figure up what you need and give me an estimate, I'll see if there's enough money available to rebuild the barn," Lily told Logan.

"I'll do that right away," Logan agreed.

"As far as the labor is concerned, Miss Lily, you know all the men who were here today fighting the fire will be back to rebuild the barn. So you don't have to worry about money for that," Roy said as he spooned the hot soup.

"But I couldn't ask them to do that," Lily protested.

"You don't have to ask them. Believe me, they'll be here when you get ready," Roy replied.

Ida May spoke up, "That's right, Lily. That's the way the country folks are. I suppose you've never been involved in anything before to realize this. And if one of them needed our help, then our men would be right there."

Lily took a deep breath and said, "That's a big relief." Then her mind went back to the fire. "Did anybody see anybody around the barn before it happened? Or was there anything in the barn to show how it started?" She looked around the table.

"No, I didn't see anyone around," Ida May told her.

The two men shook their heads. "It was too hot and dangerous in there to try and inspect the loft," Logan said.

"Maybe when the timbers have settled we can look around," Roy added.

As soon as the meal was over, Lily followed Logan out the door. She told him about seeing Thomas Hickman at the cemetery. "I didn't want to scare Violet by telling you while we were eating, but I wonder if he has anything to do with this fire," she said.

"We'll have to get up into the loft to see what happened before we know," Logan said. Then, after wishing Lily a good day, the two men turned and left.

Lily went back into the kitchen and helped clear the table. When she was done, she said, "If you don't mind watching Violet, I think I'd better go upstairs to Papa's office and see what I can find about his finances."

"Of course I'll stay down here where I can keep up with Violet," Ida May replied. "You just go on and take your time. I have some pillowcases over there that I'm embroidering, and I'll have a chance to work on them." She pointed to a sewing basket sitting on top of the sewing machine at one end of the room.

"It shouldn't take long," Lily called back as she went into the hallway.

Upstairs, she went down the corridor and opened the door to her father's office.

She opened a cupboard and saw shelves covered with papers and a row of drawers at the bottom. She had no idea where to start or what she must do. Evidently her father had just put papers in any convenient place.

"I suppose I'll have to read everything," she said.

A huge desk took up a lot of the room. "He probably kept the most important records in here," she said aloud, touching the drawers of the desk. She tried to open one. It was locked.

"What luck!" she said to herself. "Where in the world could the key be?"

She looked around the room but couldn't find a key of any kind. *That's strange*, she thought. She knew her father had carried a large bunch of keys.

Finally giving up on unlocking the desk, she took a stack of papers off the top shelf of the cupboard and sat down on the carpet to spread them out. Somehow she just couldn't take over her father's desk and chair.

The first thing she came across was the receipt for her mother's tombstone. *At least that was paid for*, she thought. She found paid receipts for seed, groceries, and tools. At the bottom of the pile were the bills for the lumber from which he had built the barn, all marked "Paid in Full."

"Nothing is in date order," she said to herself. "Some of these bills are recent, but the barn was built . . . let's see . . . five years ago. Oh, everything is in a mixed-up mess." She felt helpless as she continued to find jumbled papers in the rest of the cupboard. She couldn't even figure out whether most things were paid or not.

She figured the records on finances must be in the desk, but she had to find the key somewhere. She stood up and searched the room again, but found no key. Maybe Logan had her father's keys. She'd have to wait to ask him. He'd probably stop by on his way home that night to see if they needed anything. And Aunt Ida May would probably ask him to eat, since he lived alone in a little house at the far side of their land.

Luckily Logan did stop by late in the day and Ida May did ask him to eat supper.

When Lily asked him about keys, he said he had no idea as to what had happened to her father's keys.

"I know he always carried a big, heavy bunch of keys of all descriptions, but I've not seen them around anywhere," Logan said as they finished the meal.

"What am I going to do? His desk is locked, and I need to see what's in the drawers," Lily said with a sigh.

"Might be that I can force the lock," Logan said. "Might do a little bit of damage to the desk, but I think we could get the drawers open."

"Now, I had not even thought of that," Lily said. "I'd hate to mess up the locks, but I do need to get inside the drawers. If that's the only way we can do it, then I'd say let's do it."

Logan went upstairs with Lily to her father's office. He brought along a screwdriver and a sharp knife from the kitchen. Lily watched as he tried to trip the lock by pushing the knife through the tiny crack above one drawer.

" 'Fraid we're gonna have to jes' break the locks," Logan said, looking at Lily for permission.

"Go ahead if it has to be done," Lily told him, squinting in concentration as she watched him work to open the locked drawers.

Before long, Logan had opened all four drawers in the desk by using the screwdriver and the knife. He stood back for Lily to examine what he had done.

"You only made a few scratches, and that can be fixed," Lily said. She leaned over and pulled each drawer open and then closed it. All four drawers were crammed full of papers and record books. "Looks like this is what I need," she added. "Thank you, Logan."

"If there's nothing else, I'll run along now and leave you to do your work," Logan said. "I'll stop by in the morning to see if there's anything you need."

Lily looked at the old man with a smile and said, "I don't know what we'd do without you, Logan."

Without a word he hurried out of the room and down the stairs. Lily knew that too much appreciation made him uncomfortable.

Lily sat down and opened the top drawer on the right side. She took out the contents and put everything on the desk. These papers seemed to be in much better order.

A long time later, Lily pushed away from the desk and sat in the light of the lamp she had lit. Her head was swimming with figures. She had found his bank record, paid and unpaid bills, the deed to the property, payroll records, and just about everything else necessary to run the farm. And she was stunned to see there was very little money available. Of course, a farm had continuous turnovers from crops and stock bought and sold, but at the moment, it looked to her like they were practically penniless, considering the bank balance and the bills that needed to be paid.

There was a soft tap at the door. Lily called, "Come in." Ida May opened the door, stuck her head in, and said, "I just wanted to let you know I've put Violet to bed and I've got a fresh pot of coffee on the stove."

"Oh, thanks, Aunt Ida May," Lily said, rising from the chair and stretching her limbs. "I'm finished in here, at least for the night. Let's go downstairs and drink some of that coffee. I sure do need it."

As they sat at the table with cups of coffee, Lily told her aunt what she had found in the desk.

"It's a great mess of bills, paid and unpaid," Lily said. "And not much money. I do wish Ossie would come on home. I need to get his advice on what I should do."

"I wish I could help you out, child, moneywise, but since I'm living on the good graces of my sister and her husband, I'm not able to," Ida May said.

Lily suddenly remembered Mr. Dutton. "You know, Ossie suggested I see Mr. Dutton about a job when we talked on the ship about what I would do with my time when I got home," she said, perking up at the notion of earning money to help out. "I'm going into town tomorrow and find out if Mr. Dutton will hire me. That's what I'll do. Then I can make at least a little money to live on."

"A job, Lily?" Ida May asked. "But you don't know how to work on a job. You might could qualify as a teacher, but then Miss Potter has just been hired for that."

"Ossie said he'd probably let me work for low pay in order to give me a chance to learn something about office work," Lily said. "I don't intend working all day long, just the time of day that Violet is in school. That way I wouldn't have to worry about her."

"Are you positive a job for you is necessary? Why don't you wait and talk to Ossie, and see if he can make some sense of your father's records?" Ida May asked.

"There's no telling when Ossie will finally get home. He must have a lot of work to do in Charleston," Lily said. "And the sooner I can find something to do, the sooner I can get the money to rebuild the barn."

"Well, go ahead if you must," Ida May finally said. "But don't count on anything until you really know it's possible to get a job."

"I'll be waiting on Mr. Dutton's doorstep in Fountain Inn when he opens his office in the morning," Lily said.

As she thought about the prospect of making some money, she felt a little of the burden lift from her shoulders. Somehow she'd get their finances in order.

Chapter Twelve
Legal Notice

The next morning, after a quick breakfast with her aunt and Violet, Lily went upstairs and dressed with great care.

She chose a navy dress she had made herself in England. White piping ran around the edge of the long sleeves and a white frill circled the high neck. Tiny white buttons cascaded down the front at irregular intervals all the way to the hemline. She put on a wide-brimmed hat she had remade with material to match the dress.

She tucked her little white dress gloves in her bag and, pulling on driving gloves, she turned to look in the mirror. *Very mature and businesslike*, she decided.

Mr. Dutton's office was on Main Street in Fountain Inn. Lily pulled up her horse and cart under a tree in front of the long building that housed other businesses as well. She threw the reins over a tree limb and quickly removed her driving gloves. Leaving them on the seat, she opened her bag to pull out the white gloves and wriggled her slender fingers into them.

She stepped down from the cart and carefully straightened her long skirts. As she approached the entrance, she read the lettering on the door: "George P. Dutton Cotton Co.," beneath which was a large brass knocker. She had never called on anyone in a business office and she stared at the knocker, wondering whether she should knock or just open the door and enter.

A male voice behind her made the decision for her, "Here, let me open that door for you, ma'am."

Lily glanced over her shoulder and looked up to see a tall, handsome young man smile down at her as he reached over to the door. He swung it open wide and, removing his hat, bowed slightly and said, "After you, ma'am."

Lifting her long skirts, she stepped over the doorsill and found herself in a foyer with glassed-in partitions revealing offices beyond. She could see people working at desks inside, but they didn't seem to notice her, and she couldn't decide what to do next. She looked back at the man who had opened the door for her. He was hanging his hat on a hall tree that was standing by the door to one of the offices.

"May I help you, ma'am? My name is Samuel V. Stovall, Sam for short, and I work here," he said with a laugh that showed perfect white teeth.

"I'd like to see Mr. Dutton, please," Lily told him. She noticed his eyes were so dark they were almost black.

"I'm afraid that's impossible today. He isn't in," Sam said. "But I'd be glad to talk with you instead."

Lily became flustered and tried not to meet his gaze. "Thank you, I'll call again," she said, turning quickly to leave.

Sam rushed to open the door for her. "He's out of town, but we're expecting him back tomorrow if you'd like to return then," he said.

"Thank you, I will," Lily said, hurriedly walking through the doorway and out onto the street before he could say anything else.

She reached her cart and removed her hat and laid it on the seat. She suddenly felt too dressed up.

"Oh, Miss Masterson, may I see you a moment?" someone called from across the street.

Lily turned and looked back. An older man in a small cart had stopped and was stepping down onto the street as he waved at her. She didn't know who he was.

"You are Miss Lily Masterson, aren't you?" the man said as he came over to her.

"Yes, I am, but I don't believe I know you," she said, puzzled as to who he was. He was a plump, short man and wore a wide-brimmed hat.

"My name is Ezekiel Tomlinson, and I was just on my way out to your house when I happened to see you here," he explained. He pushed back his coat and removed a folded paper from inside. As he did so, Lily spotted a badge on his shirt.

A lawman? He handed her the paper and said, "It grieves me to do this, Miss Masterson, but I have the duty to serve this notice."

Lily suddenly felt dizzy. What was going on now? She unfolded the paper and could barely focus her eyes on the writing. "Taxes past due!" she exclaimed in disbelief.

"Yes, ma'am," Mr. Tomlinson said. "Several years worth, that is."

"Several years?" Lily asked.

"Yes, ma'am. You see, your mother was ill so long and your father had so much expense, he didn't have the money to pay the taxes. So they were allowed to slide awhile," Mr. Tomlinson explained. "But now that his estate must be settled, the taxes have to be paid or the property vacated and sold. I'm sorry but that's the law."

"I just can't believe this. My father couldn't have skipped paying taxes on our property. He just wouldn't do that," Lily argued. She looked at him and asked, "What does this mean? What am I supposed to do now?"

"Just what I said," Mr. Tomlinson said. "Either pay the back taxes or vacate the property, in plain language. They'll be selling the property if you can't pay."

"How in the world can I pay all these back taxes? I don't have any money," Lily said angrily as tears threatened to fill her eyes.

"I'm sorry, Miss Masterson," the man said. He walked briskly across the street, stepped into his cart, and drove off.

Lily climbed into her cart and held her breath to keep from crying. Her father had always taught her that tears never solved anything. She pulled the reins down from the limb and spoke to her horse, "Lightnin', let's go home." She gave him free rein, and he made his way down Main Street to the intersection, where he turned to head out into the country.

Stunned with the shock of back taxes, Lily just sat in the seat until Lightnin' pulled the cart into the driveway and stopped by the back door. Then Lily came back to reality as she saw the burned barn. Problems were cropping up faster than she could solve them, but she meant to fight every step of the way.

Logan and Roy came up the pathway from the barn as Lily stepped down from the cart. She waited for them to catch up with her and the three of them went in the back door. Ida May was sewing, and Violet was sitting on the floor playing with the puppy.

"I jes' wanted to speak to you for a minute," Logan said without sitting down. "Roy and I have looked things over, and we believe we can replace some of the timbers in the loft and put on a complete new roof, and the barn will be as good as ever."

"It will," Lily repeated. She laid the notice she had received on the table. "I don't think there's any use in bothering. Just read this," she said to Ida May, who had come across the room.

Her aunt glanced at the paper, picked it up, and read it silently. "Back taxes?" she exclaimed. "How can that be? For all those years?"

"I know," Lily said with a big sigh. She turned to the men and explained, "I was served this paper in town today. It says Papa never paid his taxes on our property for the last five years, and if I don't pay the money due, they're going to sell our property. So why bother with the barn?" She flopped herself into a chair.

Logan and Roy exchanged surprised glances.

"There must be some mistake," Logan said.

"Yes, why would your father let taxes run that far behind?" Roy asked.

"I don't believe it," Ida May said emphatically.

Lily looked at her and said, "I don't either, but unless I can come up with some proof that they have been paid, there's nothing I can do about it."

"And another thing," Ida May added. "I don't believe the taxes would have been that much."

"And all that extra charge they've added on because they say the taxes are late is ridiculous," Lily said. She rose from the chair and said, "I'm going upstairs right now and go through every paper in Papa's office to see what I can find." She picked up her hat and gloves, and turned to leave the room.

"Let me know the outcome. I'll be back here late this afternoon," Logan called after her.

Lily worked all day in her father's office. She scrutinized every scrap of paper there, but the only ones she found concerning taxes were receipts for payments made over five years before. She came downstairs at suppertime to talk to her aunt.

"The only receipts up there are over five years old," she said, sitting down near Ida May, who was finishing up some sewing.

"Well then, maybe Charlie didn't pay the taxes they claim he owes," her aunt said sadly. She stood up and folded the pillowcase she had been stitching. "Let me get supper started while we talk."

Lily got up to help her prepare the meal and said, "I'm going back tomorrow to see if I can catch Mr. Dutton in his office. If I could get some kind of job, maybe they would let me pay these taxes over a period of time."

"Maybe," Ida May said.

"I'll see," Lily replied. Then she remembered something. "You know, Logan said the timber they're cutting will bring a good price. I wonder if it would be enough to pay the taxes."

"You should ask him, child," Ida May told her.

But when Logan came by later, and Lily asked him about the timber, he said, "I'm afraid the timber won't make that much money. Besides, it's going to take lots of time to cut and sell the logs. And we've got men working that have to be paid out of whatever it brings, and it would be a miracle if we could get it all done within the time they're giving you anyway."

"I'll ask them," Lily said. "The notice has an address on it to write to if I disagree with the amount, so I'll just send them a letter and see what they say about a partial payment, as long as they know more will be coming from the sale of the timber."

She wrote the letter that night and took it to town and mailed it when she went back to Mr. Dutton's office the next day.

As much as she hated to talk to Samuel V. Stovall again, she had to talk with Mr. Dutton if it was possible. She went into the office, ready to avoid the man if at all possible. But, to her relief, Mr. Stovall was nowhere in sight. Another man came out to greet her and, after going inside for a moment, he came back to say that Mr. Dutton would be glad to see her.

And now that she was really going to talk to Mr. Dutton, she couldn't think what to say. The man led her into Mr. Dutton's office, and Mr. Dutton stood up to greet her. In one glance, Lily noticed that he was short, middle-aged, bald-headed, and blue-eyed.

"Come in, my dear lady, come in," he told Lily. "Please have a seat."

Lily sat down in the chair by his desk and he resumed sitting.

"I was terribly sad to hear about your father, Miss Lily," he said. "He was a good man."

"Yes sir, thank you," Lily replied, and then decided there was only one way to explain what she had come for. "Mr. Dutton, I'm looking for work of some kind. Ossie was on the ship with me and my sister Violet on our way back from England, and he told me I should speak to you to see if you had anything I could do." She stopped and watched his reaction.

"Oh, dear," the man said. "I'm afraid I don't have anything a lady like you could do."

Lily thought he sounded genuinely concerned, so she went on. "I know I'm not experienced in any kind of work, but if you had something I could do to learn office work, I'd be glad to work at low pay in order to get the experience," Lily said.

Mr. Dutton thought for a moment and then said, "I'm afraid there's just nothing I could offer you right now. Why don't you check back with me . . . say, next month sometime? Maybe things will change here by that time."

Lily, realizing there was nothing else to be said, thanked him and left. She would have to figure out another way to get the tax money.

When Lily returned home, she saw a strange man sitting with Aunt Ida May on the front porch, while Violet was swinging the puppy on the porch swing. Lily stopped the cart at the front and stepped out.

The man stood up and waited for her to get down from the cart. Ida May introduced the man as Mr. Stanley Jones and explained he was an investigator. He told Lily he was looking into the death of Milford Ibson, and Captain Donaldson had given him her name and address.

Lily sat down nearby and said, "Yes, Captain Donaldson told me he might send someone to talk to me."

Mr. Jones, a tall, heavyset, elderly man, replied, "We have been able to come up with enough evidence pointing to Thomas Hickman that we want to locate him. There's a good possibility he may be deeply involved in this."

Lily was surprised, and she recounted the times she had seen the man on the ship. Then she told Mr. Jones about having seen him with Wilbur Whitaker in Greenville as well as alone at the cemetery.

"I'm glad to get this information from you, because I've already spoken with Mr. Wilbur Whitaker. He told me he had not seen or heard from Thomas Hickman since they left the ship in Charleston," Mr. Jones replied. He quickly made notes on a pad.

"I know for a fact that Wilbur lied if he told you that because I definitely saw them together in that store called the Red Hot Racket in Greenville," Lily confirmed.

The man rose and handed her a card. "I am staying at this address in Greenville for a few days while I try to locate Mr. Hickman. I'd greatly appreciate it if you would notify me in case you see him again."

"I certainly will, Mr. Jones, and I hope you catch up with him," Lily told him as she rose also.

When the man rode off on his horse, Lily sat back down and explained to Ida May that she had finally got to see Mr. Dutton.

"But it was all for nothing," Lily said, repeating the conversation between her and Mr. Dutton.

"Why, that's too bad," Ida May said with a frown. She cleared her throat and looked directly at Lily. "I hope you don't mind," she said, "but Janie Belle and Aaron came by on their way to town while you were gone, and I told them about the tax notice. I thought maybe they might have a solution."

Lily looked at Ida May and said, "There just doesn't seem to be a solution of any kind."

"Well, Janie Belle did say that if . . . if you . . . have to move, you would be welcome to stay at her house—you and Violet—until y'all could do something else," Ida May said in a hurry.

Lily laughed and said, "Can you see me living with Aunt Janie Belle?"

"No, but sometimes we have to do things we don't want to do," Ida May told her. "I don't *want* to stay with Janie Belle myself, but I *have* to because of things that didn't go right for me in the past." She had a faraway look in her dark eyes.

"Like what, Aunt Ida May? What things? Tell me about it, please," Lily said as she caught a tone of regret in her aunt's voice.

"I've never been able to discuss this with anyone," Ida May said, and she nervously smoothed her full skirt with her hands. "It's something that will never go away as long as I live. It hurts even now to think about it, but I believe if I explain this to you, you'll benefit from it."

Lily looked at her aunt in alarm. She wasn't making much sense.

"What is it, Aunt Ida May?" she asked softly.

"I was once as young as you, you know, and passable in looks, though not as lovely as you," Ida May began with a deep breath. She looked out across the distant fields. "And I was in love."

"Oh, Aunt Ida May, what happened?" Lily asked.

Ida May turned to smile at her and said, "I was engaged." She paused again.

Lily, really interested now, waited in silence for her to continue.

"Papa didn't approve of my young man because he had no livelihood to keep up a wife and family, but mind you, Harry had the education. He just hadn't had time to use it. We got in too big of a hurry," Ida May explained. "Papa said we should wait, but we were young and impatient and decided to disregard his wishes."

"I remember Grandpa always seemed to favor you over Aunt Janie Belle," Lily told her.

"That was because of what happened," Ida May said. "You see, Harry and I had been to a supper for us in Anderson with some of his friends. It was on Wednesday night, and we were to be married on Saturday. We had to cross the Enoree River and—" She paused. "And we had a little grey kitten one of the friends had given us. I was holding it in my lap but when we started to cross the river, something happened to the cart and it went into the river, with us in it." She swallowed hard as her breathing became faster.

"Oh, Aunt Ida May!" Lily exclaimed.

"We were thrown out into the river, and I can't swim," Ida May continued. "And Harry wasn't much of a swimmer, but he was able to get us onto a large rock sticking up out of the water. And then he saw the kitten. It was fighting for its life against the force of the water. He managed to rescue it, but just as he set it up on the rock, something happened and the current washed Harry away. I never saw him again. He was never found. And I had no home because Papa was angry with us. So I had to go live with Janie Belle, and I'm still there."

Lily was almost overcome with the story. She moved her chair closer to Ida May's and reached for her hand. "I'm sorry, Aunt Ida May," she said. "I never realized you had such a sad past. Oh, how awful!"

"That was a long time ago, child," Ida May said as she took a deep breath. "I just wanted you to understand that sometimes you have to do things you don't want to. You might not want to live with your Aunt Janie Belle, but at least that would be a home."

Lily thought for a moment and said, "I understand what you're saying, Aunt Ida May. I know I have a place if things don't work out. But I'll keep trying to find a solution, and I won't give up until the very last minute."

"And I understand why you're trying, child," Ida May replied.

Lily gave her a hug. Just then, Lily heard Violet talking loudly out in the yard.

Lily quickly looked and exclaimed, "Aunt Ida May, it's Ossie, coming across the yard." She jumped up and ran outside to meet him.

Violet was still running to greet him, holding the puppy she had been playing with, and she and Lily reached him at the same time. "Oh, I'm so glad you're finally home!" Lily exclaimed.

"Here's my puppy I brought from the ship, remember?" Violet said as she held the little animal up.

"Yes, of course. What have you named him?" Ossie asked as he rubbed the puppy's head.

"I haven't decided yet," Violet said, and then added seriously, "I've thought about several names but nothing suits him so far."

"Well, be sure and let me know what to call him," Ossie said with a laugh as Violet ran back across the yard. He turned to Lily and put his arm around her shoulders as he said, "Roy just told me about your father. I'm sorry."

Tears came into her eyes as she looked into Ossie's. He took off his spectacles and rubbed them with his handkerchief, then grasped Lily's hand.

When they got to the front porch, Lily noticed that Ida May had gone inside the house. She understood that her aunt was giving her a chance to talk with Ossie alone. They sat down in the swing.

Lily quickly told Ossie everything that had transpired since she came home. Ossie listened until she was finished with the news about the taxes.

"Lily, I want you to listen to me for a minute," Ossie said, taking her hand in his. "So much has happened, you can't handle it all alone. I know I'm a good bit older than you, but I've always loved you since you were little. And then when you grew up to be such a beautiful young woman, I knew I felt a different kind of love for you."

Lily swallowed hard and tried to pull her hand away, but he held it fast.

"I'm asking you to marry me and let me take care of you and little Violet," Ossie continued. "I know I'm not much to look at, but maybe you could get used to being around me all the time," he added with a little laugh.

"Oh, Ossie!" Lily managed to say, tears running down her cheeks.

"You don't have to give me your answer right this minute, because I know it must be a surprise to you, but I realized on the ship that I really and truly loved you as a grown young woman, and not as a child anymore."

Lily couldn't speak. She pulled a handkerchief from her pocket and wiped her face.

"I just got home a few minutes ago, so I need to go take care of some business, but I'll come back in a little while—with your permission, that is," Ossie said. He stood up. "I'll put your horse and cart away for you."

"Yes, please come back," Lily said softly through her tears as she sat still.

Ossie walked toward her cart and horse, and when he had disappeared across the yard, Lily got up and went inside. To avoid her aunt, she went straight up the front stairway to her room. She had lots more to think about now.

Chapter Thirteen
Saved by Lightnin'

L ily walked the floor of her bedroom. She now had a solution to her problems, but could she accept it? She had never been in love, but she didn't believe she was in love with Ossie.

Then, too, what had he meant by taking care of her and Violet? Would he pay off the taxes so she could keep her own home? She doubted that, because if she married Ossie she would have to live with him in his own house. Therefore, she would still lose her home.

On the other hand, she wouldn't have to go live with Aunt Janie Belle for goodness knows how long before she could get out on her own.

And what about Violet? She needed a home at her age, a home like they had had with Papa, a happy home.

She remembered the letter she had sent to the tax people. Maybe they would take partial payments and she could find some way to earn a living.

Ossie had told her to take her time about answering his question. She decided she would wait until she received a reply to her letter before making a decision. For one thing, she didn't believe it would be honest to marry Ossie just to get a home. And besides, she wasn't sure she could love him as a wife.

So when Ossie came back after the noon meal, Lily suggested walking down to the spring.

"Let's just walk and talk awhile," she told him when he came to the back door. She looked back at Ida May, who was once again at her sewing, and Violet, who was now sitting on the floor by the sewing machine busily sewing clothes for her doll from the scraps. "If you would keep an eye on Violet, I would appreciate it, Aunt Ida May. We won't be gone long."

"Of course, child, go right ahead. And Ossie," her aunt said as she turned to him, "I'm so glad you've come home. It'll be a comfort to have you around."

"Thank you, Miss Ida May," Ossie said with a smile. "I would have been home much earlier if I had been aware of what was taking place."

Lily led the way down the pathway, which Logan always kept cleared. The grass was still green, but any day now a cold spell would probably turn it brown. As they walked, she was silent, trying to organize her thoughts.

Then Lily remembered the investigator. She decided it was better to take the subject away from her, so she told Ossie, "The captain did send a man to talk to me. And, you know, Ossie, I have seen Wilbur and Thomas here. They were both in Greenville the day Logan and I went in to see the sheriff, and on the day I went to visit my father's grave I saw Thomas leave the cemetery."

"I knew they didn't stay in Charleston after we got off the ship because they got on the train coming this way the next day," Ossie said. "Did the investigator have any more information about them?"

"Well, he did say things pointed to Thomas Hickman, and that they wanted to locate him, so I suppose that means he is guilty of something," she said as they arrived at the spring.

Her father had built a small springhouse to hold the milk and other foods that needed cooling. Lily walked around it, touched it with her hand, and then sat down on a bench made of logs nearby. Ossie followed her.

They talked for a long time, and Lily kept adding details to her earlier conversation with Ossie. He was a good listener, speaking only to confirm her beliefs about the misfortunes she had had.

"I agree that something is going on," Ossie said. "Something terrible is happening. I can't put my finger on the reason for it, but I'd say someone is trying their best to destroy you and get everything you have. I just don't understand it at all."

"Neither do I," Lily said. "I've done nothing but think about all these things ever since we came home, and I can't figure out why it's all happening. I certainly haven't done anything to anyone, so I don't know why I'm being tortured."

Ossie looked at her. As he pushed his spectacles up on his nose, he said, "I'm sorry Mr. Dutton doesn't have anything to offer you. Even a small job would help, I know."

"As soon as Logan can come up with an estimate on the timber and a date it will all be cut, I will feel a little more settled about that," she said. "And I told him not to bother with the barn for the time being, until I see how our finances look."

"I wish I had the money to loan you, for the taxes at least, but I just invested almost all the cash I have in a business deal in Charleston. That's why I was so long coming home," Ossie explained. "However, there is always another way—"

"I know, Ossie," Lily interrupted him. "I need to do some deep thinking alone."

Ossie stood up and said, "I understand. Shall we walk back to your house?"

Lily jumped up and said, "Oh, Ossie, I didn't mean you had to leave. I do my thinking in my room at night when the house is quiet and—"

Ossie interrupted her, and with a smile he said, "I know. But I really need to get back home to catch up on what's been going on over there on my place while I've been gone."

"You have been gone a long time," Lily agreed. They began walking back toward her house.

Ossie left her at the back door, saying, "I'll catch up with you tomorrow between my work and yours." He smiled, gave her hand a little shake, and walked across the yard toward his house.

"See you then," Lily called to him.

Lily went back upstairs and tried to make some order out of her father's office by sorting and separating paid bills and unpaid bills that afternoon. She stacked the bills that seemed to be outstanding on top of the desk to ask Logan about. He could explain what they were for and would have an idea as to whether or not they had been paid. Maybe her father had just not added the receipt to the bill.

So when the old man stopped by late in the afternoon, Lily took him upstairs to go through the bills.

"I know you have always known what Papa was doing businesswise, so I would like to ask about these things," Lily told him as they sat down together by the desk.

Lily patted a pile of papers and said, "These are all bills for food at Todd's store, and none of them are marked 'paid.'"

"No, they wouldn't be," Logan said. "You see, your father would always get whatever he needed, jes' sign for it, and then pay Mr. Todd when he had cash money coming in, like the timber he just recently sold. He collected for that and probably paid bills with the money after he paid the help."

Lily was beginning to understand how a farmer lived. "So then Mr. Todd would know whether these are paid or not, wouldn't he?" she asked.

"That's right and if you'd like for me to take them, I've got to go down there tomorrow and pick up a list of things that Miss Ida May says you need," Logan said. "And I could inquire about these then."

"That would save me a lot of time if you could, Logan," Lily said as she pushed the papers toward Logan. "There's probably a clean, empty flour sack down in the pantry you could put these in."

As they continued through the stack of papers, Lily was glad to hear that a lot of them had been paid. There were still a few items outstanding, such as chicken feed and seed grain for the crops. Logan explained that things like that weren't usually paid until the chickens were sold or the crops planted and there was money to turn over.

After a while, Ida May tapped on the door to say supper was on the table. They were almost finished, so Lily stood up and said to Logan, "We can go through the rest of them tomorrow, or whenever you have time. Let's go eat now."

Logan followed Lily and Ida May down to the kitchen, but he protested, "You know, I don't come by here to get free meals. I know very well myself how to cook. I only stop by when there's something I need to see you about or to check on y'all and be sure y'all don't need something." He stood in the middle of the floor.

Ida May looked up at him and said, "Oh, hush up! We like having company at meals, and not only that, it saves you time." She gave him a little push. "Now get over there and wash up, and don't let me hear you talking like that again."

Logan looked at her in surprise as he walked to the sink and said, "Yes, ma'am, Miss Ida May."

"After all, Logan, you are like one of the family," Lily added. "You've been around this place longer than I have." She laughed.

As soon as the meal was over, Lily said, "I think I'll saddle up Lightnin' and go for a ride. He really needs some exercise."

Logan looked at her as they all got up from the table and said, "In that case, I'll go get him for you."

"Thanks, Logan," Lily said. She and Ida May began clearing the table. She looked up at the tall, old man and said, "I wasn't hinting at that. You do so much work, I don't want you waiting on me when it's something I know how to do for myself."

"Oh, now, you've got to help Miss Ida May clean up the kitchen, and I'll have him saddled and waiting by the time you get through here," Logan said, going quickly out the door.

And Logan *was* waiting outside with Lightnin' when Lily finished. She walked down the pathway to the driveway, where her horse stood.

Logan watched her as she stepped on the mounting block and swung herself up onto Lightnin's back. He said with a frown, "Now, don't you be goin' too far from home this time of day. The days is getting shorter, and dark will be coming soon."

"I won't," Lily promised, and she leaned forward to stroke the horse's neck. "And besides, Lightnin' knows the way home." She shook the reins, and Lightnin' moved on down the driveway. Logan called to her, "I'll wait till you get back."

"Now, why does he have to wait until I get back?" Lily said to herself as the horse carried her onto the road.

She knew where she was going, but she didn't want to talk about it to anyone. Her father's blacksmith shop was her destination. She wanted to walk around there by herself and think about her problems.

When she got there, she loosely tied Lightnin' to a hitching post and looked around. She picked up her father's hammer, which he had left lying there. She put it back down and ran her hand over the top of the anvil—smooth iron, now cold to the touch. She stooped to pick up one of the horseshoe nails nearby. Papa had always told her nails should never be left around. And then she found a half-made horseshoe lying behind the furnace.

"He must have been working on this," she said softly to herself as she examined the piece of iron. She squeezed it tightly in her hand and walked over to the storage cabinet. Her father had kept supplies such as nails and small tools in it.

She opened the doors and looked inside. It was well-stocked. She closed the doors, and something fell from the rafters overhead and almost hit her. She jumped back and looked down to see what it was. There, lying at her feet, was her father's bunch of keys.

"Papa's keys!" she cried excitedly as she stooped to pick them up.

"Nothing doing," a male voice said angrily from behind her, and Lily was given a shove that sent her sprawling onto the floor. A booted foot stepped on her hand as she reached for the keys.

She cried with pain and tried to pull her hand out from under the man's foot. "Let me go!" she cried angrily. "Stop it!"

"Not until I have the keys," the man replied, pinning her down from behind.

With her free hand, she reached for the piece of iron horseshoe that had fallen out of her grasp with the sudden attack. She quickly grabbed it and, with all her power, hit the man's shin.

The man instantly cried out in pain and moved his foot. Lily withdrew her painful hand, managed to get to her feet, and looked up to find Thomas Hickman jumping around and rubbing his shin. She was instantly afraid for her life. Quickly backing away from him, she headed for her horse.

"Lightnin', let's go home!" she screamed. The horse immediately pulled loose from the hitching post and came in her direction.

As she reached to catch the reins and mount up, Hickman caught up with her and grabbed the back of her skirt.

"Help! Help!" she cried at the top of her lungs. She was swinging to hit him with the unfinished horseshoe she held.

Lightnin' reacted to his mistress's cry and turned on the man. He reared up and kicked Hickman down before the man knew what was happening. Then her horse started stomping, and Lily suddenly realized Lightnin' would kill the man if she didn't stop him.

Looking down at the man, who was unconscious, she talked to her horse as she took the reins and persuaded him over to the mounting block. Lightnin' didn't want to obey, but he did. Lily swung onto his back, gave him free rein, and screamed, "Home, Lightnin', home!"

The horse quickly reacted and carried Lily at a speed at which she had never ridden before. She clung on and prayed they would reach the house in one piece. Lightnin' was fast, but he was also smart. He knew that he had his mistress on his back and that she was in danger.

In a few minutes, the horse braked in the driveway to her house with such speed that the dirt started to fly under his feet. Lily sat up and pulled on the reins. "Good boy, Lightnin'," she called to him as she jumped down and tied the reins over the post.

Logan and Ida May were both standing in the yard by the time she dropped to her feet. Not only that, Ossie and Roy had evidently heard the commotion and they were rushing across the yard toward her.

Lily tried to get her breath. "Thomas . . . Hickman . . . tried to kill me . . . over at Papa's shop," she said between gasps. "Lightnin' attacked him. He may be . . . dead." She sank to the ground because her legs would no longer hold her up.

Without a word, the three men raced to Ossie's barn to get horses. Lily watched and tried to calm herself down. Ida May stooped beside her and said, "Come in the house, child. They'll see to that man." She reached down a helping hand.

Lily accepted her support. She got up and went into the kitchen. Sinking into a chair by the warm iron cookstove, she remembered part of her pain was coming from her injured hand. She needed help but was past speaking. She held up the bruised hand to Ida May.

Her aunt gasped and rushed around the room getting warm water to bathe it and liniment to rub on it. "Oh, dear, what happened?" Ida May asked. "Are you injured anywhere else, child?"

Lily shook her head as she looked at the scratched palm of her other hand.

Ida May carefully examined the injured hand. "Thank the Lord it's not broken," she said as she tied a bandage around it. Then she got a pan of clean water and washed Lily's face.

Lily was silent all the time, and her aunt looked at her with concern. "Are you all right, dear? Should we send for the doctor?" she asked.

Lily shook her head and said, "No, I'll be all right when I get over the shock." She reached for the washcloth and wiped her face again as the tears came.

Ida May sat down next to her and waited. Lily finally straightened up and was able to explain what had happened.

"I found Papa's keys," she began.

Her aunt was shocked.

Lily repeated the whole story when Ossie returned alone.

"He'll be all right," Ossie told Lily. "He's not going to die.

Logan and Roy are taking him into town, to the jail." He reached to lay her father's keys in her lap. "Evidently he had these."

Lily took the keys and held them close with both hands. It was then that Ossie noticed the bandaged hand and he looked up at Ida May.

"It's not broken," Ida May explained. "Bad bruise but no broken bones from what I could tell—and she didn't want the doctor."

Ossie looked back at Lily and said, "We'll see how it is in the morning."

Lily told Ossie and Ida May everything she could remember.

Ossie stood up and walked around the room. "Thank the Lord you had Lightnin' with you," he said.

"Yes, and you know, I've never seen Lightnin' so upset," Lily said. "Why, he would have killed the man right then and there if I hadn't stopped him. And you know, Lightnin' was tied up to the hitching post when Aunt Ida May found my father. Do you think he could have tried to protect my father, but someone managed to tie the reins? I'm sure if there was anything violent, Lightnin' would have became raving mad and would have done everything he could to stop it."

"That's a possible idea," Ossie agreed. "Lightnin' has always seemed so gentle, but you know now that he can be dangerous, too."

Logan came back later to tell them that Thomas Hickman was locked up, and word had been sent to the sheriff in Greenville to come and get him. The jailer in Fountain Inn had known about the investigator looking for the man.

"Well, I sure hope they don't let him out where he can come back down this way," Lily said with a catch in her breath as she moved her hand, causing it to throb. "Is Lightnin' all right?"

"Oh, yes, I put him up for you in my barn," Ossie told her. "He's fine."

"I'm so thankful that man didn't have a chance to injure Lightnin'," Lily replied.

* * *

Things were calm for the next few days. Then Lily received a reply to her letter regarding the taxes. Her offer was flatly refused. Time was running out for her to vacate the property.

"Well, I guess I'm at the end of my rope," Lily told Ida May as she sat reading the letter to her aunt.

"Now that's no way to talk," Ida May rebuked her. "You and Violet have a home with Janie Belle. Don't forget that."

"I should go over and talk to her," Lily said. Her hand was not bandaged anymore, but it was black and blue with bruises, and so sore she couldn't use it. "Soon as I can get this hand working again, I'll go."

"When they came by the other day, she said that they would come back, so maybe she'll show up again," Ida May said.

The next day a letter came from Mr. Stanley Jones, the investigator. He gave Lily all the facts now known in the case since Hickman had been captured.

"Aunt Ida May, Mr. Jones says Mr. Ibson had a lot of money in his room on the ship, and it has been proven that Thomas Hickman stole it. In fact, Thomas Hickman got the room numbers mixed up somehow and he was the one who broke the lock on our room, thinking it was Mr. Ibson's," Lily told her aunt as she sat reading the long letter.

"And to think you and Violet were in danger all that time!" Aunt Ida May exclaimed, pulling her chair closer.

"They have determined that Thomas Hickman had a fight with Mr. Ibson and either killed him and threw him overboard or injured the man enough that, when he was thrown over he couldn't save himself! How awful!" Lily said.

"And what about this Wilbur Whitaker, his friend?" Ida May asked. "Does Mr. Jones say anything about him?"

Lily scanned the pages of writing and said, "Wilbur is not guilty of anything. He says, in fact, Wilbur was trying to dissuade Thomas from doing all these things." She looked up. "I do remember them having an argument in the dining room and Wilbur getting awfully angry, and he kept on saying, 'I won't do it.' So I suppose Thomas was trying to get him involved in his wrongdoings."

"I'm thankful you were not injured more than you were," Ida May said.

"So am I," Lily said with a faraway look in her blue eyes. "Well, at least some things are working out."

But her immediate problems were still there.

Chapter Fourteen
Decisions

L ily did a lot of thinking during the next few days. The sheriff had never come out to see her, and she was determined she would talk with him. The problem was that she could go all the way to Greenville and not find him in again. So she put it off.

And she had the urgent matter of trying to save her home looming before her. There seemed to be nothing she could do but accept Aunt Janie Belle's offer and move into her house. Lily was grateful for the offer, but she couldn't bring herself to accept it. She kept hoping something would happen to save her home.

And as far as Ossie was concerned, Lily knew she couldn't marry him, yet she put off telling him that. Not another word had been spoken between the two about this. She knew Ossie was giving her time to decide.

She was glad Thomas Hickman had been captured. Every time she looked at her hand, which was gradually healing, she had cold chills thinking about what he had tried to do to her at the shop.

Lily thanked Aunt Ida May daily for staying on and helping out with Violet and the house.

Violet still refused to name the puppy. She claimed she

couldn't think of an appropriate name. The child was completely occupied with the little animal. He still slept in her room at night because Lily hadn't the heart to banish him downstairs.

One morning, Violet and the puppy were outside when the little animal's loud barking caused Lily to look out the doorway. Aunt Janie Belle and Uncle Aaron were just pulling up in the driveway. Lily went out to greet them.

"Come in, Aunt Janie Belle, Uncle Aaron. I'm glad to see y'all," Lily said, and Ida May came down the pathway behind her.

Janie Belle didn't say anything until she had maneuvered her large body out of the cart and onto her feet with Uncle Aaron's help.

"Well, since y'all haven't been back to see us, we thought we'd better check on you to see if y'all are still alive," Janie Belle said, frowning as she walked toward the back door.

Lily grabbed Janie Belle's hand and stepped in front of her. "I'm sorry, Aunt Janie Belle," she said. "I just don't seem to be thinking straight lately with so much going on. I should have been to visit you, I know."

"Well, I suppose you'll be moving in with us soon anyway," Janie Belle said as they continued into the kitchen.

Violet had followed, carrying the puppy, but she stood back, looked, and listened to find out what was going on.

"I've tried everything I know and I can't seem to come to a solution," Lily said as they sat in chairs at the far end of the kitchen.

Uncle Aaron finally spoke. "You get these men that worked for your papa to start bringing your furniture over to the house," he said. "We can put it in the attic for the time being. And the other things, tools or whatever, you can put in our barn. We've got plenty room, so I don't know what you're waiting for. Soon'll be cold weather."

"Thank you, Uncle Aaron," Lily said gratefully. "I'm so thankful."

"Then let's get moving," Janie Belle said from the rocker she sat in.

Violet had backed up against the cupboard, but now she stepped forward and asked, "Are we moving in with Aunt Janie Belle and Uncle Aaron?" She frowned as she looked at Lily.

"Would you like to go live with Aunt Janie Belle?" Lily asked her.

"Can I take my puppy?" Violet asked, still holding tightly to the little animal.

Lily looked at Janie Belle, who smiled and said, "Of course, child. And you know what? There's a tiny white kitten that's taken up at our house. We don't know where it came from, but you can have it, too, if you'll feed it and look after it."

Violet's blue eyes grew round in excitement as she asked, "Is he like Snowball? Mandie Shaw's cat?"

Aunt Janie Belle didn't understand what she was talking about, but Lily answered, "If he's white, he must look at least a little like Snowball."

"Can I go get him right now?" Violet asked.

"Not right now," Lily said. "We have lots of things to do before we can go stay with Aunt Janie Belle."

"Who is Mandie Shaw?" Janie Belle asked Lily.

"She was a girl we met on the ship when we went to England, and she had a white cat named Snowball that Violet took up with," Lily explained.

"Will you keep the kitten for me until we get there?" Violet asked.

"Of course, child, but you need to hurry up and get moved," Janie Belle said.

Violet looked at Lily and said, "We will hurry, won't we, Lily?"

"It won't be long," Lily told her.

Violet seemed satisfied with the answer and she ran back out into the yard with the puppy.

Ida May stood up and asked, "Why don't we move over to the table? I know there's coffee in the pot."

Aunt Janie Belle and Uncle Aaron followed Lily to the table as Lily pulled out chairs for them. Then they sat down.

"I'll get the cups," Lily said across the room to Ida May at the stove.

"Better get some cake plates, too," Ida May said. "I'll get the rest of that chocolate cake that I baked last night out of the safe."

Lily laughed and said, "I'm sure there couldn't be much left with Logan, Ossie, Roy, and Violet all loving chocolate."

While they ate cake and drank coffee, they all recalled memories of Lily's house. It was the old homeplace for Mastersons way back at the beginning of America, and Lily's father had renovated it when his father gave it to Charlie and his new bride.

"It's bad that the place is going out of the family but Aaron and I have talked and we've decided there is no way we can help you save it, so the only thing for you to do is just move in with us—lock, stock, and barrel," Aunt Janie Belle said.

"They can't take anything but the house itself and the land," Uncle Aaron informed Lily. "So plan to move everything else over to our place."

"There's something I haven't even thought of before, but how could I have overlooked such an important matter," Lily said. "What about Logan? I know Papa gave him that little house to live in, but was it done legally? What I mean is, can they take his house, too, because it's on our land?" Her heartbeat quickened as she thought about the old man being out of a home.

The others looked at each other in question.

"Lily, seems to me like it was my papa who gave that to Logan, and not yours," Janie Belle told her. "And I seem to recall that it was done at the time he was dividing up the property between his children and my papa was still living here in this house, and Charlie was not yet married."

"Oh, I hope so, Aunt Janie Belle," Lily said. "How can we find out for sure?"

"Well, just ask Logan. He ought to know," Janie Belle said. "Now, we've got to be on our way into town to fetch a few things we need." She stood up and pulled her shawl around her tightly.

The others rose also, and as her aunt and uncle left, Lily promised them that she would begin preparing for the move.

"I know it has to be done, and I am so thankful for y'all," Lily said. "I haven't been able to start packing, but I will today." She felt her heart flip over as the reality came before her.

She stood in the yard and watched till her aunt and uncle drove out of sight down the driveway to the road. Then she walked down the pathway, stopping to stare at the burned barn. She had anger in her heart. If she was not going to be able to keep her home, why hadn't that barn just burned up and shot a flying spark onto her roof that would have burned her house up as well. She didn't want someone else living in her house, the house where Papa, her dear mother, and her grandfather had lived. It belonged to her. How could she let someone else take it away?

She sat down on the grass and cried for a long time.

Suddenly she heard Violet calling as she ran toward her, "Lily! Lily! There's a man—two men—up at the house, and Aunt Ida May told me to tell you they want to see you."

Lily raised her head and wiped her eyes on the apron she still had on from working in the kitchen that morning. She didn't want Violet to see her crying, so she spoke without looking at the child, "Men? Do you know who they are?"

Violet immediately came around in front of her and looked at Lily with serious eyes. She asked, "Do you hurt, Lily?"

Lily reached forward and pulled the child down into her lap as she hugged her tight. She didn't answer the question, but she whispered, "I love you. I love you, my dear little Violet."

Violet put her small arms around Lily's neck and kissed her on the cheek. "I love you, too, Lily," she said, and then squirmed to get up. "And Aunt Ida May said to hurry."

Lily was slightly alarmed with that remark. Who were these men? She got to her feet and walked after Violet, who was now running back toward the house.

As she went up the pathway, Lily saw a fancy rig standing in the driveway. Two men, one older and the other younger, were talking to Aunt Ida May. As Lily came closer, she realized with alarm that the younger man was Wilbur Whitaker. Now what did he want? And who was the older man with him?

Wilbur saw her coming and stepped across the yard to meet her.

"How are you?" he asked, just as though nothing had ever happened before—the talks on board the ship and the question he had asked about coming to visit her once she was home. Lily tried to fight the excitement she felt at seeing him again. He really was attractive, but he had a mixed-up personality.

Lily just looked up at him but kept walking until they reached the place where the older man was talking to Aunt Ida May. The other man was short, overweight, redheaded, and blue-eyed, with lots of wrinkles on his face and lots of grey in his hair.

"Lily, this is Mr. Whitaker," Ida May began to introduce them. "And his son, Wilbur."

"Mr. Whitaker? Wilbur's father?" she asked in surprise.

"Yes, that's right," Mr. Whitaker said. "Now, I came out here to discuss a little business with you."

"Business? What kind of business?" Lily asked. She was determined she was not going to invite them into her home.

"I just wanted to take a little look at your property, if you please," the man explained. "I understand it'll be up for sale soon."

Lily gasped. Anger flooded her face so strongly she couldn't speak.

Ida May explained, "He says they are already advertising it in town, Lily."

"Who is advertising it in town?" Lily asked when she could breathe again.

"Why, the officials who will be foreclosing on you for unpaid taxes, if I may be so blunt," Mr. Whitaker explained. "Now, if you don't mind, I'd like to take a look inside the house and around."

Lily put her hands on her hips and said, "You get off my property! It's not for sale yet! Now, get!" She was so angry, she couldn't see straight.

Mr. Whitaker looked at her and said, "Well, what I had in mind was maybe buying it from you before you lose it."

"I said, 'Get off my property!' " Lily screamed at him. "Do I have to go get Papa's shotgun to show you I mean *get*?"

Mr. Whitaker looked at her again and, with a sneer, he said, "All right, we'll go. But I warn you that you will be sorry." He turned to walk back toward the rig.

Wilbur seemed to hesitate as he watched Lily. He stepped in front of her and said, "You should listen to my father, Lily. Please. I talked him into coming here and making this offer so you would at least have something left over from the sale."

Lily looked at Wilbur for a moment before she spoke. "Just what does your father want with my property, when you said your family was so rich? Surely he wouldn't be planning on living here. What are y'all up to now, Wilbur?"

"I'm sorry, Lily. I guess I just can't make you understand," Wilbur told her. "My father buys up property for investment. He wouldn't want to live here."

"Well, this house and land are not for sale yet, so you get off it, too," Lily said.

"I'll go now, but I'll be back," Wilbur said, turning to join his father at the rig.

Lily stood there staring at them until they drove off and out of sight. Then she turned to Ida May who had stayed by her side. "Vultures!" she muttered.

"I know you're upset, Lily, and this is going to be an awful ordeal, but you have to realize someone will buy your property," Ida May said, and then holding up her hand, she added, "Now let me finish. And after I've said what I intend, you may want to ask me to go home. But, Lily, have you forgotten there is a God who takes care of you? When have you asked Him to help you?"

Lily instantly embraced her aunt and said, "I'm sorry, Aunt Ida May. I have asked Him to help me, but He doesn't seem to be doing anything about it. Things just get worse and worse. I'm going to lose the house and land, and I can't find any way to earn money to live when I'm gone from here." Her voice trembled.

Ida May held her close and said, "Just give Him time, Lily. Give Him time."

As they walked back to the house, Lily was silent as she thought about what Ida May had said. Had she lost her trust in the Lord? Had she allowed earthly things to occupy her mind? To make her angry?

As they entered the door into the kitchen, Ida May told her, "Now we probably should leave this room to the last to pack. Suppose we begin with the bedrooms?"

Lily blinked her wet eyes and stared at her aunt. Yes, packing was going to have to begin. She nodded and said, "All right."

That night, while Lily and Ida May were sitting at the end of the kitchen, Violet was playing with the puppy by the cookstove. The night air had begun to be chilly, and the fire was still going in the stove.

Ossie suddenly knocked on the door, and Violet, when she saw Ossie, jumped up and ran to meet him as Lily opened the door. "We're getting ready to move everything out of this house and put it in Aunt Janie Belle's attic and she has a white kitten waiting just for me," she told him excitedly. "Lily and Aunt Ida May have already packed up some of the bedrooms upstairs."

Ossie looked at Lily with a sad expression. "Then the answer is 'no,' I suppose?" he asked.

Lily felt the hurt that he must have felt. "I'm sorry, Ossie, I just couldn't do it for that reason. If I . . . thought it was something deeper, I would say 'yes' in a minute," she tried to explain without letting Violet know what she was talking about.

"If you ever change your mind, would you promise to let me know?" Ossie asked in a low voice, standing perfectly still before her.

Lily nodded and said, "I promise, but I do care for you, Ossie, like I always have—as a big brother." She straightened her shoulders and tried to smile. "Now, come on in. I'll put on a pot of coffee." She glanced over at Ida May, only her aunt had left the room. Violet was playing with the puppy.

Ossie followed her to the stove as she prepared the coffee.

They sat at the table while it percolated. They looked at each other silently. Ossie took off his spectacles, wiped them with a handkerchief, put them back on, adjusted them on his nose, and finally looked back to Lily.

"I hope our friendship will continue like it's always been," he said.

Lily reached to pat his hand. "Of course, Ossie," she said. "I just have to be sure I love the man I marry—that is, if I ever marry. And I have to work out my future. I may have to move out of here now and give up my home," she patted her heart, "but I feel right here that the good Lord will help me get it back some day." As she spoke, Lily realized her trust was strong in the Lord again.

"Mr. Dutton told me that you had been in and that he was sorry he didn't have anything at all to offer you but that he would keep you in mind if anything comes up in the future," Ossie said. "He's a man of his word. He'll be in touch if he can give you any work."

"Thanks for telling me that, Ossie," Lily said. "I had not counted on ever hearing from Mr. Dutton again, but maybe I will. In the meantime we'll be staying with Aunt Janie Belle and I'll be waiting and watching for a solution to our future, mine and Violet's."

The puppy ran across the room to Ossie's feet. Violet followed. Ossie bent to pat his head. "What have you named him, Violet?" he asked.

Violet shrugged and said, "Nothing yet. I haven't found a proper name for him." She picked up the puppy and took him back over by the cookstove.

Ossie smiled and Lily said, "He just has to have a name."

Across the room, Violet heard that remark and she said, "Don't worry about it. I'll find a name for him one day."

Ossie and Lily both turned their heads to keep Violet from seeing them laugh.

After a cup of coffee, Ossie went home and Lily told Violet it was bedtime. As the child carried the puppy up to her room for the night, Lily wondered what would happen at Aunt Janie

Belle's if she did that. Life was going to be different. They would be in someone else's house and would have to abide by their rules.

Lily started to pick up the coffee cups when there was another knock on the door. She wondered, *It's bedtime. Who could this be?*

She opened the door and found Logan standing there. "Come on in," she told him.

He stepped inside and said, "I just wanted to ask you something. The men have been working late, but I needed to know . . ." He stopped and looked at her.

"Here, sit down. I've got coffee already made," Lily told him. She hurried to the cupboard for a clean cup, filled it, and then refilled hers before she sat down with him at the table. "Now what did you want to ask me?"

"I know you're getting all packed up and everything," Logan began and, clearing his throat, he asked, "I just wanted to know if you would like for me to clean out your papa's shop and pack it all up."

Lily's breath caught. She had not even thought of that. "Oh, Logan, I'm glad you asked me," she said. "I might have just moved out and left it all there." She paused, and he waited. "Yes, I'd like for you to do that for me. I'd appreciate it. And if you could just take it on over to Aunt Janie Belle's, she'll show you where to put it." Lily shut her eyes and drew a deep breath.

"I'll do that tomorrow then," Logan said without looking at her. He held his coffee cup with both hands.

Then Lily remembered she had something to ask him. "Logan, when Aunt Janie Belle and Uncle Aaron were here this morning," she began, "we talked about you, about whether you own your house and piece of land outright, or will these people take it, too?"

Logan looked at her and said, "Don't worry about me, Miss Lily. Your grandpa gave me the deed, free and clear of everything. Those tax people can't touch it. I pay my own taxes."

"Oh, I'm so relieved!" Lily exclaimed. "I suppose you've already heard we're moving in with Aunt Janie Belle, just for the time being, though."

"Yes, I run into Ossie, and he told me jes' a little while ago," Logan said.

"You ran into Ossie? Then you must have met up with him when he left here a little while ago," Lily said.

"In fact, to be truthful, Miss Lily, I met him on the pathway, and we stopped to talk a minute. He was real worried about something," Logan said. "Then he said you had made the decision to move in with Miss Janie Belle."

"For the time being," Lily said, breathing deeply to steady her voice. "Just long enough for me to figure out where we're going from there."

"Are you moving the livestock?" he asked.

"I have to get everything off the land, so I'd appreciate it if you'd just let the stock stay at your place, since you had already moved it there when we came home. I may have to sell some of it later," Lily said.

"There's not much there. Your papa had been selling off a lot of it," Logan told her. "I believe I'd jes' keep what's left till you decide what you're gonna do. You can always use the milk and the eggs, even over at your aunt's house."

"I haven't really talked to you about what we had since I came home," Lily said. "But you're right. We'll just hold on to it for the time being."

Logan stood up. "Guess I'd better be getting along," he said. "I've got the men coming at the crack of dawn. We're trying to get all that timber cut before anyone notices."

"Before anyone notices?" Lily asked, rising from her chair.

"Well, I don't exactly know what the law is, but they might forbid you to cut any timber if you're not going to catch up the taxes," Logan told her.

Lily gasped in shock. "You mean we shouldn't be cutting that timber? The time is not up yet for the property to be sold," she said quickly.

"I've heard sometimes they don't allow you to, what they call, *depreciate* the property, and that would include cutting timber. But, mind you, I don't know that this is the case with yours. All I do know is that we're gonna work day and night and get that timber cut before anyone knows any better," Logan said.

"What would they do to us if we aren't supposed to be doing that?" Lily asked.

"Since neither one of us has any money, I don't know what they would do. I suppose they could try to collect for the sale of the lumber from whoever bought it," Logan said. "Anyhow, don't worry your head over it. I'll take care of everything." He walked to the door, where he took his hat from the peg he had hung it on. "I'll talk to you tomorrow. Good night." He opened the door and went out.

Lily stood there wondering. Were they breaking some kind of law cutting their own timber on their own land? She didn't think so. She just hoped they would be finished by the time she had to vacate the property.

Lily waited until the last day she was allowed by the law before she began moving. Then people came from all over the countryside to help. And in one day's time, the house stood empty after generations had occupied it.

Lily kept busy running back and forth between her house and Aunt Janie Belle's, so she wouldn't have time to think. Finally everything was moved, and Lily and Violet, with Ida May's help, set up their bedrooms with their own furniture in rooms that Aunt Janie Belle had cleared out for them. Violet had the puppy and the little white kitten under their feet the whole time, but Lily didn't say anything about it. The child would have trouble adjusting to her new home with Aunt Janie Belle.

Lily walked the floor all night in the new room. She didn't even take off her clothes because she knew she wouldn't sleep. As she thought about the busy day, she had a strong urge to go back for one last look at the house, the house where she was born, the house where her mother had died and which her papa had owned.

"No use, no use," Lily told herself. "There's no use in going back to look at an empty house. I'll just try to remember it like it was."

When morning finally came, Lily freshened up and slipped

out of the house. She would go for a ride—somewhere, just anywhere, to think. She found Lightnin' behind Aunt Janie Belle's fence and he came to her, but as she stood there, she realized she had responsibility now and couldn't just go riding off somewhere.

"Later, Lightnin'," she told her horse. "We'll go for a ride later."

While talking to Lightnin', she saw a horseman come riding down the road and she waited to see who it was. He turned into Aunt Janie Belle's driveway and jumped down to tie up his horse.

"Why, it's Logan!" she said aloud to herself as she hurried over to speak to him. "Good morning, Logan."

Logan turned around quickly and said, "Mornin', Miss Lily. I jes' wanted you to know we jes' pulled the last log off your property. We made it."

Lily reached for his old wrinkled hand, looked up into his tired face, and said, "Logan, I thank you with all my heart."

Logan smiled, patted the top of her head, and said, "Better get back in the house now. It's right chilly out here this time of the morning. I'll let you know what kind of transaction we can make on the timber."

"Thank you, Logan," Lily said again. Logan mounted up and rode away, waving back to her. She went back inside to warm up. It was chilly outside.

The day was confused for Lily and Violet, being in a strange place and with other people. Time seemed to drag as Lily felt helpless now to take care of herself and her little sister.

Then in the afternoon, things changed. Lily was sitting on the front porch steps, watching Violet play with the puppy and the kitten in the yard, when someone rode up in a rig, stepped down, and walked toward the house.

The man looked familiar at a distance, but she couldn't remember where she had seen him. Then, as he came closer, she recognized him as the man who had served the paper about the past due taxes. She frowned and held her breath. He recognized her and came to the steps.

He tipped his hat and said, "Good morning, Miss Masterson, I just wanted to give you this." He held out a folded piece of paper.

Lily stood up, backed away from him, and stared at the paper.

"It's just a courtesy copy of the sale of your property," the man explained. "Just wanted you to know that it was sold."

Lily snatched the paper, unfolded it, and quickly read the contents. She looked at the man and said, "This says Mr. Whitaker bought my property. How much did he pay for it?"

"It says right there on the paper, for the amount of back taxes," the man told her, pointing to the number on the paper.

"What a bargain for him," Lily said, turning to walk up the steps to the porch.

The man got back in the rig and drove away.

Ida May came out the front door. "What did he want, if I may ask, child?" she said as she came out onto the steps.

Lily handed her the paper, rubbed her eyes, and said, "It's for real now. Mr. Whitaker bought my property." She sat down on the top step.

Ida May read the paper and then she excitedly asked, "Lily, did you notice his lawyer's name on here, the man who witnessed his signature? Look!" She held it down for Lily's inspection as she pointed out the line.

Lily glanced at it and jumped up excitedly. "Weyman Braddock! So Weyman Braddock is Mr. Whitaker's lawyer! And he's the one who sent the message and the fare to come home!"

"I would say, dear, that it was done in order to get you home so they could serve the papers on you to take the property. It might have been a long, drawn-out matter if you had remained in England," Ida May told her.

"Yes, this explains a lot of things," Lily agreed. She was silent for a moment and then added, "But it's all over. There's nothing I can do about it."

"It is all over now," said Ida May. "You need to look to the future, to a happier future, and if you keep your faith you'll find a better time."

"I know," Lily said. "I believe that, too, Aunt Ida May." She folded the paper and put it in her pocket.

Everyone had just finished supper that night but they were still around the table when there was a knock on the front door.

"I'll see who it is," Ida May said, getting up and going out of the room.

In a minute she was back. "It's that investigator, Mr. Jones, to see you, Lily. I asked him to wait in the parlor."

"He may have more information about Thomas Hickman," Lily said, and she left the room.

When she entered the parlor, Mr. Jones stood up and said, "I apologize for calling this late, but I had trouble finding you. Then Mr. Creighton, next door to your house, explained where I could find you. I'll only take a minute of your time."

"Do sit down, Mr. Jones. I have plenty of time," Lily said. She waved him to a chair and sat down across from him.

Mr. Jones was fidgeting with the inside pocket of his coat, but when she sat down, he finally pulled out a large envelope and offered it to her. "This is for you," he said.

Lily hesitated. Every time she accepted a paper it was bad news. But she had met and talked to Mr. Jones before, and she couldn't imagine what kind of paper he was offering her. But she finally accepted it.

She looked at the large envelope with her name "Miss Lily Masterson" written across the front. It felt thick. There must be several papers *inside*, she guessed.

"Go ahead, open it," the man urged her.

Lily glanced at him and then ran her thumbnail under the flap to break the seal. She glanced inside and saw several sheets of white paper, which she pulled out. She slowly unfolded the paper. It was a letter addressed to her. Rapidly scanning the contents she gasped in surprise.

"A reward? For me?" she exclaimed, looking up at Mr. Jones. "But I didn't do anything to deserve a reward."

"That letter shows Mr. Ibson's family's thanks for your help in capturing Thomas Hickman, who has now been found guilty of the poor man's murder," Mr. Jones said. "And of course the money is coming from Europe so that will take a while."

"But I don't know those people," Lily said. "I can't take those people's money."

"But, Miss Masterson, those people want to express their thanks, and you really should accept the reward," Mr. Jones told her. "I have no idea as to how much it will be, but I'm sure the family is well off and can afford to do this."

Lily considered that for a moment. "Well, I suppose if I refused it they would think I was rude."

"That's fine," Mr. Jones said, and he stood up. "Now, I am assuming it is all right to give them the address to send the reward to."

"Yes, sir," Lily said as she followed him to the front door. "And I thank you. I appreciate your trouble."

"All part of my job," Mr. Jones said, walking through the outside door. "Good night, Miss Masterson."

Lily closed the door and leaned back against it. She glanced at the papers in her hand. These people were going to give her some money. She wasn't sure she deserved it, but she was going to accept it. Any money at all would be a help.

" 'Ask, and it shall be given you,' " Lily quoted the verse Aunt Ida May had said to her. "Thank you, dear Lord. I don't know how much it will be but I thank you for giving it to me."

She went back into the dining room to explain to the others that a miracle had happened.

"I have been thinking a lot lately, and I believe if I can get enough money to set up a dressmaking business, I can make money at it," she said. "And this reward, whatever amount it is, will be the nest egg for it."

It had all come to her in a flash while she was explaining who the visitor was—she could earn a living in dressmaking. She was sure of it.

Dear Reader:
 Please—

NAME THAT DOG!

Send your suggestion to:

Lily's Fan Club
P.O. Box 5972
Greenville, S.C. 29606